MURDER AT ᴛʜᴇ HUNTING LODGE

A 1920S HISTORICAL COZY MYSTERY - AN EVIE PARKER MYSTERY BOOK 11

SONIA PARIN

ISBN: 9798516407468

CHAPTER 1

Havoc in the Boudoir

Halton House, 1921

*B**reathe in, hold, exhale...*
Evie kept her eyes closed and focused on being in the moment, perfectly unencumbered by the chaos swirling around her and floating on a cloud of bliss. A cloud sparkling with a silver lining, she mentally amended. Focusing, she drew in another deep breath filled with contentment and emptied her mind.

Caro's recent close call with an assailant had shaken Evie to the core.

Following Tom's suggestion, she had delved into the

mysteries of Eastern Philosophy and Meditation. And, after reading the first book on the subject, which she'd found tucked in a corner of the library, she had immersed herself in all things meditative, finding moments throughout the day to practice quietening her mind and emptying it of all frivolous thoughts.

At first, she had expected it to be easy. However, after a minute of silence, her foot had gone to sleep. So, she'd had to straighten, stretch and rearrange herself in a comfortable position.

With the help of some humming, she'd found her way back to a soothing flow of quiet emptiness. However, regardless of her intense focus and determination, it hadn't exactly been smooth sailing.

When her nose had itched, she'd told herself to ignore it. But the itching had persevered. So, she'd argued with herself saying it would only take a second to scratch and then she could resume her meditative journey. But a part of her had insisted she needed to master the skill and overcome those intrusive twitches and superfluous thoughts weaving in and out of her mind and ignore everything else that demanded her attention.

In the end, she'd caved in and scratched.

On that first day, she'd struggled with several distractions, but she'd held on to her stalwart determination, battling with each one until she'd emerged victorious.

The technique of emptying her mind of all disruptive thoughts and diversions had now taken hold of her. Even after several weeks since she'd first looked into the idea of quietening her mind, she had remained diligent, practicing every day, usually in the library and, sometimes, in the bathtub.

Evie swept her hand across the soapy surface.

Breathe in, breathe out—

Caro's shriek punctuated the sound of glass hitting the floor and shattering.

Startled and curious about the sequence of events, Evie looked over her shoulder, leaning slightly to see past the Japanese screen used to block drafts.

Had the shriek come before the fall?

"I'm perfectly fine, milady," Caro called out. "The same can't be said for your scent bottle. I'm ever so sorry…"

Evie lowered herself into the tub and held the rose scented soap against her nose. Lately, Caro had been all fingers and thumbs, not to mention absentminded. While being entirely too focused on—

"What will Henry think? I mean, what would he think if he could see me now?"

Henry.

Henry Evans.

Evie released a long breath.

Detective Inspector Evans had been courting Caro for several weeks and the relationship appeared to be progressing quite rapidly. Any day now, Evie expected to be overwhelmed by an explosion of joy and she would lose her maid to marital bliss and that would leave her in the hands of…

"*Millicent!* Always lurking around the corner waiting to see me fall flat on my face," Caro complained.

"I am doing no such thing, you ungrateful girl. Can't you see I'm here to help you clean up the mess you made?"

Most ladies, Evie thought, aimed for an heir and a spare. While she had settled for a lady's maid and a spare. And, lately, for reasons unknown to her, they had both become as rambunctious as two-year-old children.

"Her ladyship is right next door and she can hear every word you say," Caro admonished in a harsh whisper.

"She knows who the troublemaker is," Millicent informed her. "I have a good mind to warn the detective about you, but he's my only hope of ever getting rid of you."

Caro stomped her foot, her exasperation rising above anything Evie had ever heard from her maid before.

"For your information, I have no intention of giving up my position here."

Millicent harrumphed. "Her ladyship won't stand to have a married lady's maid. You'll be shown the door as soon as you say *I do.*"

"That only goes to show how little you know her."

Evie knew she should intervene and call for calm but she'd had days of this type of behavior and no amount of reasoning had worked. It almost made her believe the earth had fallen out of alignment, with all the petty troubles in the world converging at Halton House. She really had no idea what had come over her maids.

She heard her bedroom door open and confident, determined steps making their way into her room.

Millicent gasped. "Mr. Winchester, her ladyship is in the tub and she's not to be disturbed."

"That's not your job to say," Caro complained.

Evie didn't hear Tom's response. However, seconds later, she heard her maids scurrying out of the room.

She waited a moment and, when she felt silence had been restored, she resumed her meditative breathing technique.

Breathe in, breathe out.

Heavens!

Evie sighed. "Tom, did you scowl at Caro and Millicent? You know how sensitive they can be. Especially Millicent. You'll give her nightmares." Glancing over her shoulder she saw him leaning against the doorframe, his eyebrows drawn down into a dark scowl as he studied a piece of paper he held.

"Apologies for interrupting, Countess. Should I come back later?"

"No, that's fine. I will endeavor to carry my state of calmness into... my conscious state, or something along those lines and deal with whatever calamity you are about to share with me. Out with it. What's troubling you?"

He lifted his hand and waved a letter at her. "This has to stop."

"Oh, heavens. What is it now?"

"Your grandmother."

"Toodles? Surely, not Toodles." She'd always appreciated her granny's grounded steadiness and practical outlook.

"No, not Toodles. Henrietta."

Yes, she supposed Henrietta was her other grandmother.

"She has that Barclay Chides fellow wrapped around her little finger. He follows her everywhere and hangs on her every word. And, worse, he does her bidding without question and this is the result."

Barclay Chides, the young man the Dowager Countess had engaged to track down Tom's forebears had been staying at Halton House for several weeks now using it as his headquarters to organize his various research activities.

Tom growled under his breath. "When is he going to get it through his thick head I am descended from thieves, cutthroats and wh—"

Evie raised a halting hand. "Do please spare me the sordid details. Besides, you do tend to exaggerate. I thought he'd found a clergyman in your line."

"Oh, yes. The Reverend Ignacio Winchester who settled in New Amsterdam in the late 1600s. My first transgressing forebear. He killed a man with a single shot. Apparently, he used to bless his bullets."

"Tom, those were wild times, I'm sure. And you

know stories like that abound. Even right up to the late 1800s, half the continent remained quite wild with people taking the law into their hands in order to survive." Evie held the rose scented soap against her nose again and then lathered her hands. "You knew what you were up against when Henrietta showed up with Barclay Chides, and yet you didn't stop her. Instead of indulging her, you should have nipped the idea in the bud." Evie smiled as she recalled how Tom had looked cornered and ensnared. She had imagined him praying for the earth to open up and swallow him whole.

"Have you ever tried to stop Henrietta?" he complained. "She doesn't have a bee in her bonnet. She has a head full of bees. Yes, an entire beehive."

"Dear, sweet Henrietta," Evie hummed. "You know she means well."

Tom snorted. "This obsession she has with finding me a title has gone far enough."

Evie agreed. Most people would say Henrietta belonged to a different generation. However, rank and circumstance remained an obsession with everyone, especially those in the higher circles of society.

"What's in the letter?" Evie asked, her voice full of innocence.

"Mr. Chides has been in touch with my relatives back home and they are overjoyed at the idea of having a family member with a title. They want to know when they can come over and stay in my castle because, of course, the title comes with a castle."

Evie couldn't resist the temptation. "Does it?"

Tom growled, "You know very well there isn't a title," his voice hitched, *"or a castle."*

"So, what do you want me to do about it?"

Tom straightened and crossed his arms. "We need a distraction." He gave a stiff, determined nod. "Yes, that's what we need. Something to take their minds off this business of a title because, of course, it's not just Henrietta. She has the others all wound up too."

"Toodles and Sara? Surely not." Evie could imagine her grans teasing and indulging Henrietta for her own amusement but Sara, her mother-in-law, normally chose to be more moderate and down to earth.

"I know you're thinking there's no real harm done." Tom huffed out a breath and brushed his hands across his face. "My apologies, Countess. I should not be burdening you with this petty annoyance."

Why would Tom take this to heart? Usually, he laughed at Henrietta's antics. In this instance, she would most likely meet with failure. Surely, he had to know that. Could Tom be concerned about that? Did he secretly wish for Henrietta to unearth a title that would elevate him and put him on the same social level, right alongside her?

A few years back, Consuelo Vanderbilt had separated from the Duke of Marlborough and Evie knew for a fact they were about to divorce, clearing the way for Consuelo to marry the man she had fallen in love with, a man without a title. She didn't have any qualms about discarding all the privileges of her rank.

Tom had to know the lack of a title didn't make a difference to her. Truth be known, she had been entranced by Tom Winchester since the early days when he had pretended to be her chauffeur.

"She's not just digging up my past in the hope that she'll find a distant relative here in England. She's now moved on to, or rather, reverted to what she refers to as *Plan A*."

"Dare I ask?"

Tom roared, "She will get me a title by hook or by crook."

Evie scooped in a breath and, instead of easing it out, she huffed it out. Heavens! Why couldn't everyone just be happy? It seemed the moment someone lifted a finger to do something, it affected the person next to them and, in turn, their actions affected the next person.

She thought she heard Tom issue another murmured apology which only made Evie more aware of his frustration.

Tom had never been one to complain, not really. In fact, out of all the people in her immediate orbit, he could always be relied on to provide a sense of calm and steadiness.

Had he succumbed to the chaos plaguing Halton House?

Evie nodded. Yes, something needed to be done. The sooner, the better.

CHAPTER 2

Order in the house

The drawing room

*E*vie leaned her elbows on her writing desk and cupped her chin in her hands.

She had no idea why everyone had been behaving in such an erratic manner. Recently, she had agreed to join Lotte Mannering's lady detective agency and had assumed this would make everyone happy.

Instead, they were all acting strangely and some were even on edge, including the cook, Mrs. Horace, who had been over seasoning all the meals.

Heavens, despite being fully engaged in her

endeavor to find Tom a title, even Henrietta's behavior had been odd, appearing at Halton House at the oddest moments and for no apparent reason, waltzing into rooms only to leave them without offering a word of explanation.

Then, there were the housemaids…

As she'd made her way downstairs, Evie hadn't been able to shake off the sensation of being watched. And she hadn't imagined it. Twice, she had looked over her shoulder and had seen housemaids peering at her from around the corner. This unusual behavior had made her wonder if Henrietta had finally succeeded in engaging the services of spies.

She tried to avoid thinking about the constant bickering she'd been hearing because that would lead to worrying about the servants being unhappy.

Evie hoped all this chaos hadn't been brought about by her lax attitude. Some would say she had allowed everyone too much freedom; sweeping away the lines of demarcation which, in other households, kept everyone in their place.

Indeed, this type of behavior wouldn't be tolerated in other households. But what could she do about it? Hope everything would return to normal by itself?

She didn't want to bring it to Edgar's attention. If she did, she knew he would deal with it by saying something along the lines of *"Now then, there'll be no more nonsense."* And that would be the end of that.

Or would it?

Evie silently groaned.

Maybe everyone had been affected by something else. Something in the air. A premonition of change.

Caro's life would certainly change soon. While, from the conversation she had overheard, her maid had no intention of giving up her position, Evie thought she might change her mind after a while.

Would Caro be happy continuing on as her lady's maid? Other people working as servants had been changing their lives by leaving service to work in factories or even training to work in offices.

She wondered if Caro might be interested in pursuing another line of work. Marrying a detective, she might even want to join Lotte's agency. Yes, Evie could certainly see her doing that. Especially since, a while back, she had expressed an interest in doing just that.

In any case, Evie didn't think her husband would want her to continue working as a lady's maid. She hoped this wouldn't cause trouble between them. However, if Caro wished to continue working, there might be something else she could do within the household.

While married women were expected to stay home, she had heard of some women pursuing careers.

Perhaps she could create a new job for Caro. After all the years they had known each other, it would be a shame to lose contact with Caro. Yes, indeed. If she wished to continue working they could put their heads together and come up with something.

She put the matter aside for the time being and focused on the problem at hand.

Casting her admiring and surprisingly calm gaze toward the expansive view of the park, Evie listened to the murmured conversations coming from the other side of the door.

She knew Edgar, her butler, had been standing outside the drawing room for at least ten minutes. Evie had asked not to be disturbed and, it seemed, Edgar had taken it upon himself to guard the room against intruders.

A few minutes before, he had been joined by Toodles who had quizzed him about her activities that morning. Evie hadn't heard her granny walking away so she assumed she remained standing outside the door, possibly curious to see what would happen next.

A moment later, Evie heard tiptoed steps tapping along the wooden floor followed by more hushed whispers. It took her a while to identify the interloper, succeeding only when said interloper sneezed.

Millicent.

Evie heard the door handle turning and the door opening a fraction only to be closed abruptly. She assumed Edgar had stopped Millicent from barging in.

Next came Caro and she made no effort to disguise her approach.

The hushed whispers rose in volume and were followed by a light tap on the door.

Caro breezed in with a confident and cheery greeting, "Sorry to disturb you, milady. I thought you might be chilly in here since no one has tended to the fire since early this morning."

Evie replied with a hum and resumed her letter writing. Signing her name, she folded the piece of paper and slipped it inside an envelope.

"Would you like me to take those letters, milady?"

"Not yet, Caro. I haven't finished my correspondence." Taking another piece of paper, she began writing another letter. Keeping the missive short and to the point, she signed her name, and repeated the process. Sealing the envelope, she added it to the growing stack of letters.

While Caro's furtive glances did not go unnoticed, Evie refrained from looking up. On any other day, she might have imagined her maid had drawn the short straw and had been sent in to spy on her. However, under the current strange circumstances, she knew there had been a power struggle between Millicent and Caro, and Caro had simply burst into the room.

"Mr. Winchester has been asking about you, milady. At least, that's what Edgar said, but he didn't wish to disturb you because you seem to be rather busy... with... something or other."

Evie waited a moment. When she felt sure her maid would remain silent, she set her pen down and erupted to her feet, in the process, startling Caro who flung her arms out and yelped.

Evie heard a rush of footsteps scrambling toward the door and she imagined Edgar and the others pressing their ears against it.

"Are you quite all right, Caro?" Evie asked, her tone calm.

With her eyes wide and her mouth gaping slightly, Caro gave a vigorous nod. "Perfectly fine, milady."

Instead of fussing over Caro and apologizing for startling her, Evie turned back to her desk and collected the letters, smiling as she heard Caro breathe a sigh of relief.

If they insisted on behaving erratically, then she would match them.

Indeed, she would outdo them.

She might even succeed in outsmarting them.

During the last few days of unrelenting upheaval in the household, when reason had failed to restore peace, she'd tried to ignore everything happening around her. Since that hadn't worked, she had settled on a different course of action, involving secrecy and silence, with a hint of disapproval as well as indifference.

Evie turned and handed the letters to Caro who looked down at them almost as if not knowing what to do next.

Since each envelope had a name and instructions to deliver them on a specific date written on it, Evie assumed Caro would know what to do with them.

She thought her plan would only work if she kept Caro in the dark so she fought the urge to chat with her. "I'll be in the library and not to be disturbed. Is that clear?"

"Y-yes, milady. I'll make sure of it... Even if I have to stand guard at the door myself."

Before she reached the door, Evie heard a confusion of footsteps which receded toward different directions.

Opening the door a fraction, she found the hall empty. Heavens, even Toodles had hurried away. "Silence isn't just golden," she murmured, "it's also powerful." They were all probably wondering what she'd been doing behind closed doors. And they would continue to wonder until they received the letters she had just composed.

Satisfied with how much she had achieved by doing practically nothing, Evie crossed the hall and entered the library.

"Countess," Tom said distractedly. "There you are." He set his newspaper aside and gave her his full attention. "What have you been up to?"

Walking toward him, she cast an appreciative glance over a display of blooms on a table. "I've been busy organizing everyone."

Amusement shone in his eyes. "Including me?"

Up to a point, Evie thought, relieved to see him in a better mood—amused rather than frustrated.

He added, "I should apologize again for unloading all my petty annoyances on you earlier." He shifted in his seat and smiled at her. "I actually meant it to be a lighthearted complaint. Nothing serious."

"There's absolutely no need to apologize. Everything has now been sorted out," Evie declared.

Sounding surprised, he said, "You've hatched a plan."

Yes, Evie thought and prayed it wouldn't backfire

on her. Evie sat down next to him. "Pack your bags, Mr. Winchester. We are leaving."

His eyebrows hitched up. "For good?"

"Honestly, Tom. Henrietta will eventually tire of her project and find something else to occupy herself with. However, I hate to see you looking so miserable. So, I've arranged for the lodge to be opened up."

"The what?"

"The Woodridge hunting lodge. It's up north. I instructed Mr. Miller, the caretaker, to open it up. I haven't been there since... well, since before the war, which means you haven't been there either. It's a lovely house. If you're not keen on shooting, there's also fishing and, of course, horse riding."

"How is this going to take Henrietta's mind off me?"

"You and I will leave today." Seeing his surprise, she nodded. "Yes, you'll need to pack quickly." She glanced up at the clock and thought Caro would be opening her letter right that minute with the instructions to pack for a trip, no other explanation offered. "I have worked out an itinerary. It should take us a couple of days to drive up with stops along the way. Then, in a few days, everyone else will follow by train."

"They're coming with us?"

Evie smiled at Tom's surprise. "I'm afraid so. But they'll have a few days to wallow and ponder the error of their ways. I'm hoping our absence will put an end to everyone's erratic behavior."

"Does your plan include losing Mr. Barclay Chides

along the way? Because, otherwise, I don't see how this will stop Henrietta."

"Rest assured, Mr. Chides will be busy."

Tom grinned. "Indeed."

"Yes, indeed. He will be receiving a letter soon from someone claiming they are researching their family history and they have stumbled upon a certain Mr. Winchester who traveled to America many years ago and established a dynasty. This Mr. Winchester is presumed to be a second son of a titled gentleman who sought his fortune in the new world. The family writing to Mr. Chides has been struck with one tragedy after the other and they are now in desperate need of an heir."

When Tom spoke, he sounded awestruck, "You baited him?"

"I merely gave him a tiny false lead to follow. It should keep him busy for a while chasing his tail."

Tom studied her for a moment. "You masterminded this for my sake? I thought you said I was making too big a deal of it."

Once again, Evie wondered why Tom objected to Henrietta's research. Perhaps he just felt uncomfortable being the center of attention. Or maybe there were far more rascals to be unearthed than even he'd been willing to admit to and he feared she might be discouraged or put off altogether.

She gave the idea some thought only to dismiss it because it would require Tom to think poorly of her and she knew for a fact he admired and appreciated her. No matter what Mr. Chides discovered about his past, Tom had to know she would never take such nonsense seriously.

"This serves several purposes," Evie continued. "I have no idea what has come over the servants and everyone else. For a brief moment, I falsely believed I had everything... everyone under control..."

Tom laughed. "But then you started misplacing your riding crop."

"Precisely. It's not exactly the most elegant accessory." She gave him a brisk smile. "Anyhow, the trip will offer everyone a diversion. Also, or, rather, more importantly..." She dug inside her pocket, "I have received a most interesting letter from Lotte Mannering. The timing, of course, is perfect." She handed Tom the letter and sat back to watch him read it.

When he finished, he looked up and frowned. "When did this arrive?"

"This morning. That's when I barricaded myself in the drawing room to design an effective course of action." The lady detective had received a plea for help from someone who worked at Lynchfield Manor and she'd thought Evie would be interested in looking into it.

Tom read the letter again. "I assume Lynchfield Manor is near your hunting lodge."

She nodded. "Lotte can't join us because she's on another case. We'll be on our own."

"Does that mean you want to keep the others in the dark?"

She had no idea if her tactic would work. Evie shrugged. "I thought it might be easier to keep things simple this time. I rather like my plan. In fact, it all worked out quite well. After reading Lotte's letter, all the pieces fell into place. Following the directions Lotte provided, I located Lynchfield Manor on the map and realized it was within driving distance of the hunting lodge. So, I decided we could all do with a trip there. Leaving the others behind will only make matters worse. If they come with us, they won't suspect a thing. Anyhow, once they arrive they might become curious about our whereabouts since we will be driving out to investigate this matter. I am hoping they'll think we are out and about exploring. I'm also hoping that since we'll be departing first, they will have a few extra days to calm down so they might not even question our absence."

Seeing Tom's look of confusion, Evie sighed. "Does that sound too complicated?"

"For your sake, I do hope they mellow. In reality, I don't see it happening. In any case, how do you hope to gain access to Lynchfield Manor? Do you know the owners?"

"There's only one owner, he's a widower in his seventies. Viscount Bertram."

"You'll have to refresh my memory. What do we call him?"

Evie sat back and gazed up at the ceiling. "You'd think this would be second nature to me by now. Let me see... When we first meet him, as I'm sure we will, he'll most likely introduce himself as Viscount Bertram and we'll call him Lord Bertram or, if he encourages it, Bertram." Tilting her head in thought, she repeated the name several times.

Frowning, she searched her mind. Did she know him?

The more she thought about the name, the more familiar it became. She dug deeper and tried to remember if she had met him. It would have been at a shooting house party. Since he lived nearby, he would have come for the day.

A horde of people traipsed through her mind. Too many to name. The hunting lodge had been quite popular during the season with guests trekking up from all over England.

"I'm sure it will come to me. Probably when I'm standing face to face with him."

"Pardon?"

"Oh, I'm just thinking out loud."

Tom tapped the letter. "What about the person who contacted Lotte? Lotte didn't include any information about her."

"Alice Brown," Evie hummed and dug inside her pocket. "You're right, Lotte didn't include much information about her but she did mention a meeting place." She produced the second part of the letter. "Alice Brown has seen a photograph of us in the newspaper so she will approach us."

"It sounds very mysterious."

"I'm inclined to agree." Tilting her head in thought,

she added, "For a moment, I wondered if Lotte might be trying to test us."

"You think she set this up?"

"It's possible. It would be easy enough to do." Narrowing her eyes, she leaned forward and peered out the window. "Good heavens."

Tom turned in time to see someone ducking. "Is that…"

"Yes, Henrietta. She was spying on us."

CHAPTER 3

Meanwhile, in the Countess' bedroom...

"It's just not right," Millicent complained. "Her ladyship shouldn't be going off who knows where without a lady's maid. Who will help her dress and do her hair?"

Caro put away the letter she had just read for the second time. "The instructions are clear and you will do well to be quiet and just carry on with your duties. It's not our place to question her ladyship."

"It's just not right," Millicent insisted. "She should take me. I did a fine job of looking after her in London while you were visiting your parents." Millicent lowered her voice to add, "Then you came back and snatched the position from right under my nose."

"I heard that and I did no such thing. I was her ladyship's maid long before you came along. You're only here because she took pity on you."

Millicent hauled the trunk off the bed and set it down on the floor. "What did she write in your letter?"

"Probably the same thing she wrote in yours. We should do as we are told and bicker to our hearts' content while she's away."

"She can't be serious."

"She most certainly is. She wants us to…" Caro unfolded the piece of paper and read the line again. "She wants us to purge ourselves of bickering. Or else we will both be out on our ears without a letter of recommendation."

"She doesn't mean that."

"Probably not, but we'll never know. I for one intend to do as I'm told. If you wish to test her, then, by all means, go right ahead."

"I still think you should give up your job," Millicent grumbled. "You already have your man. It's like having your cake and eating it too."

"It's still early days. Besides, Henry hasn't proposed yet."

Millicent gave her a bright smile and encouraged her by saying, "You should be a modern girl and propose to him."

Caro slammed her hands on her hips. "What nonsense and now that I think about it, you have your man too. Why hasn't Edgar proposed to you? What's wrong with you?"

Millicent clucked her tongue. "We want a long engagement."

"So, you are engaged!"

"I didn't say that."

Red-cheeked and out of breath, they both huffed out a breath and collapsed onto the bed.

"Bickering is hard work," Caro complained.

Millicent agreed. "And not much fun when we're being disagreeable on purpose. I don't even understand how it all started."

Caro couldn't put her finger on a specific time, especially as she'd always chided Millicent for being too chatty. Her scolding had never been mean-spirited. Lately, however, they had been getting carried away. Before becoming lady's maid to the Countess of Woodridge, she had been employed in the Duke of Hetherington's household, taking care of Lady Constance, the Duke's younger sister. Sadly, she had succumbed to the Spanish flu. Left without a position, she had been lucky to be rescued by her ladyship. Caro felt she owed her everything, including her loyalty.

In this new world they were all living in, doors were opening everywhere and she knew she had the ability and opportunity to pursue a new line of work. However, she loved her position working in a grand house. Now more than ever since her ladyship had introduced such an element of excitement into their lives.

Caro remembered the fun she'd had the first time

she had appeared as Lady Carolina Thwaites, her ladyship's cousin thrice removed.

Where else could she enjoy playacting such a fantasy?

"I feel we've taken advantage of her ladyship," Caro admitted. "She's been ever so kind to us. We wouldn't get away with this sort of behavior in another household."

"Yes, we have it as good if not better than Lady Astor's maid," Millicent agreed. "Although, she gets to travel first class. I hear she even travels to America with Lady Astor."

Caro waved her letter. "This is an ultimatum. I'm not going to test her ladyship." Sitting up and straightening, she said, "Come on. We have a lot of bickering to get out of our system."

Before they could dive into another verbal fray, the door opened and two footmen walked in.

"What are you two still doing here?" One of the footmen looked at his watch. "The trunks are supposed to be ready." Digging inside his pocket, he produced a piece of paper. "It says right here. Collect luggage at one."

"They're ready, but..." Caro and Millicent were both wide-eyed, "what did her ladyship write in your letter?"

"That's for me to know and for you to mind your own business. She'll be up here in a few minutes to change for her trip."

Caro uncrumpled the letter she had shoved inside

her pocket. "She will not be needing any assistance." She must have read the line a dozen times but its meaning had not quite registered in her mind. She looked up. "What does that mean?"

Millicent shrugged. "It looks like her ladyship thinks you're superfluous." She tipped her head in thought. "Or is it redundant?"

"In that case," Caro growled, "you have also become redundant."

"Oh." Millicent's lip quivered. "This is all your fault."

Caro grabbed Millicent by the hand and dragged her out of the room. "Quit your whimpering. I can't bicker with you if you cry."

"I don't like this game anymore."

"Nor do I but her ladyship knows what she's doing. Pull up your socks or you'll find yourself listed in the *Lady*. Although, without a letter of recommendation, you'll be lucky to be allowed to post a card at the local postal office. Now, hurry, before her ladyship comes up to change for her trip."

Millicent gaped at Caro. "So, it's true. They are leaving without us. Do you really believe they're going to the hunting lodge?"

"We won't know until we get there," Caro snapped. "Good heavens. Our very existence in this household depends on us making ourselves scarce and you're still quibbling."

As they rushed out of the room they encountered Edgar. The butler stood at the top of the stairs reading a letter. When Caro saw him looking at his watch, she groaned, "Her ladyship means to keep the entire household on the hop and too busy to stick our noses where they don't belong."

~

The next day... the dower house

Sara, the Dowager Countess of Woodridge, took a leisurely sip of her tea. "I fail to see what all the fuss is about."

Henrietta scoffed at her daughter-in-law's insouciance. "Why do you always insist on taking everything in your stride?"

Surprised by the observation, Sara smiled. "Because I refuse to be alarmed. Evie and Tom obviously wish to be alone. You must admit, we are always underfoot. One must remember they are a young couple wishing to enjoy each other's company without the constant presence of prying eyes."

"Evangeline hasn't exactly exiled us from her presence. We will be joining her in a couple of days. What do you make of that? What is the meaning of the timing?" Henrietta demanded.

"Quite simply, they wanted a few days alone," Sara insisted. "Why is it so difficult to understand and accept?"

"As far as I know there is only a caretaker at the

hunting lodge. How will they manage? What will they do without servants?"

Sara dismissed the concern with a wave of her hand. "Perhaps they have made other arrangements."

"You seem to forget how close the hunting lodge is to the border and to Gretna Green."

Sara laughed. "Have you been reading *Jane Austen* again? These are modern times. Young people do things differently now. If Evie and Tom wish to settle matters and marry straightaway, they don't need to go to such extremes."

"You seem to have changed your tune. A few weeks ago, you were prepared to join them on their honeymoon."

"Yes, well... I have come to my senses. Perhaps you might want to try it."

Bradley, Henrietta's butler, entered the morning room and announced, "The Countess of Woodridge's grandmother."

"In other words," Henrietta said, "Toodles."

Bradley's cheeks colored.

"Go on, say it," Henrietta encouraged. "If the Halton House servants can do it, so can you."

Henrietta's butler took a deep swallow and stammered, "T-Toodles."

Evie's grandmother, Toodles, took a tentative step inside the morning room. "Can I come in now?"

Henrietta nodded. "I must apologize for my butler. He is a stickler for formalities."

Toodles breezed in and sat down. "Have you both opened your letters?"

Henrietta pointed at the missive on the table. "We have indeed and we were just discussing what it all means."

Sara picked up her letter and glanced at it. "Henrietta is determined to read between the lines. I've tried and I can't for the life of me find a hidden message."

"And are we going to abide by her request that we remain here for two more days and then travel up to the hunting lodge?" Toodles asked.

Sara and Henrietta glanced away.

"I see. Birdie has tamed you overnight."

Henrietta thrust her chin out. "Until Seth comes of age, Evangeline remains the head of the house." Looking impish, she smiled. "I must admit, for the past few weeks, we have been stirred into naughtiness. Sometimes, I struggle to remember what we used to do before Evangeline's return to England."

Sara nodded. "We used to lead hectic social lives with one engagement after the other. I look at my diary now and see nothing but blank pages. I now realize we have put ourselves at Evie's disposal."

Henrietta grinned. "That's because Evangeline offers a greater diversion."

Toodles helped herself to a cup of tea. "Henrietta's right. Birdie is the one who introduced an element of adventure and we can't help getting carried away with it all. This might be her way of drawing a line on the sand."

"Are you saying she wishes to exclude us?" Henrietta could not have looked more appalled.

"I'm not entirely sure that is her plan," Sara mused.

"I know my granddaughter. Birdie means to put us in our places. We have been rather intrusive. Also, let's not forget the incident with her maid, Caro. I've never seen Birdie looking so concerned. I imagine she feels responsible for our wellbeing and fears we might come to harm."

"I'm inclined to agree with Toodles, up to a point." Henrietta nodded. "I don't think she means to keep us out of her investigations. We are far too valuable."

Sara adjusted her cup on the saucer. "We have been taking her generosity for granted and pestering her with our constant presence. I insist this is about Evie wanting time alone with Tom."

Toodles set her cup down. "Next you'll be saying I have overstayed my welcome."

Sara chortled. "Why would I say that? We stopped wondering about your departure some time ago, my dear."

Toodles stared at Sara without blinking then said, "So, you are both going to sit here and wait for your scheduled departure."

"What else is there to do?" Sara asked.

Shaking her head, Toodles rose to her feet. "I'm returning to Halton House to pack."

They watched Toodles leave. After a moment of stunned silence, Henrietta said, "What do you suppose she meant by that? Why are people so intent on saying and doing things which are open to all sorts of inter-pretation?"

"We must do something." Seeing Henrietta's state of confusion, Sara clarified, "I think Toodles took excep-tion to my remark. What if she intends to return to America? We must stop her. What will Evie think? I'll tell you what she'll think. She will blame us for her grandmother's sudden departure."

"If her intention is to sail away, I really don't see what we can do to stop her. What if she actually means to go to the hunting lodge now instead of waiting? Do you suppose that's what she means to do?"

Sara worried her bottom lip. "She will have given Edmonds instructions to drive her to the station. I suggest sending someone over to Halton House."

Urged by the need to take immediate action, Henri-etta rang the small bell she kept near her. When her butler appeared, she said, "Send someone over to Halton House and stop Toodles from leaving by any means you deem necessary."

CHAPTER 4

That sinking feeling weighed down by regrets

Two days later
The Woodridge Hunting Lodge

Sometimes, Evie thought, the most sensible solutions were not the best ones to pursue.

She had wanted to remove herself and Tom from everyone's bizarre behavior at Halton House because she'd thought that would solve the problem.

While she had, at first, tried to reason with everyone she now viewed her solution as turning her back on the problem.

Did she really believe her absence would mellow everyone's mood?

Heavens, of course not! She had probably made the situation worse. And now she had to deal with the gushing torrent of guilt assailing her.

She knew her actions didn't reflect the depth of affection she felt for her family and for those who worked for her.

How could she have left them to their own devices, departing in such an abrupt manner with no explanation?

At this point, Evie laughed.

She considered the scene taking place right then at Halton House and didn't go further than picturing Edgar tied up in a chair and subjected to a severe inter-rogation and forced to reveal all because, of course, they would all assume he harbored privileged information.

Too late now to alter her plans, she thought and decided she would find a way to make it all up to them.

After washing off the dust from their last leg of their journey, Evie made her way to the hunting lodge drawing room where she found Tom. As she entered, she cast her gaze around the room filled with small ornaments added over the years, mostly by previous generations.

Light spilled into the room through tall windows draped with thick velvet curtains. Two high-backed upholstered chairs were arranged by the stone fireplace with other pieces of furniture scattered around the room.

Of the two drawing rooms in the hunting lodge, this one had always been used as a private one to spend quiet moments away from the guests before retiring for the evening.

Evie headed straight for one of the chairs by the fireplace. Seeing a familiar cushion tucked into the corner, she smiled and recognized it as her one and only attempt at embroidery.

Tom stood facing the fireplace, his hand leaning on the mantle, one foot resting casually on the fender. He appeared to be deep in thought.

When Evie sat down, she set the cushion on her lap and ran her hand along it. All those years ago, when she had first married, she'd had to find her way through the labyrinth of her new life, which had included new routines and new customs. Sara had offered a guiding hand while her husband, Nicholas, had provided solid support insisting she had the liberty to make or break the rules.

Not the rules of etiquette, Evie thought. They had been ingrained in her from an early age. Some things were simply written in stone. Of course, he had been referring to the aspects of her new life that might not quite fit in with her preferences. In his opinion, if she didn't want to spend time at the hunting lodge, she didn't have to. She remembered making a joke about him wanting to get rid of her so soon.

Since he'd brought up the subject, she'd taken the opportunity to leave him in no doubt of her intentions. She had married into the aristocracy and she had every intention of fulfilling her role by emulating his mother and grandmother.

His breath had gushed out and he'd looked appalled.

Despite being a young bride, she had interpreted his reaction and had assured him she wouldn't emulate them all the time, of course.

"Home," Tom murmured. "Someone felt happy enough about the hunting lodge to embroider that."

Emerging from her reverie, Evie laughed. "At the risk of exposing myself to ridicule, I will admit this is my work. I labored over the first word but then gave up on the rest. It was supposed to read *home sweet home.*"

"So, this place holds fond memories."

"Oh…" Evie smiled as she recalled the moment she had set down her sewing needle. Nicholas must have noticed her struggling with the wretched thing and that's when he'd told her she could do as she pleased because, of course, she had been expected to spend part of her time enjoying gentle pursuits such as embroidery. Ironically, the expectations had also included developing a passion, if she hadn't already, for blood-thirsty sports. "Yes, it does hold fond memories. The hunting lodge has always invited a sense of relaxation. We used to come up several times a year, sometimes alone, then to get the horses fit for the hunting season, and then to open up the house to guests wishing to do some shooting and hunting."

Tom straightened a framed photograph. "Have I missed something? Is this the shooting season?"

"No. We are definitely out of season." Evie turned her attention to the fireplace. "If you think about it, it's all mapped out. August marks the opening of grouse season. We'd always head up north to Scotland for that. September is partridge shooting followed by pheasant season in October." Evie shuddered. "In those days and even now, I always avoided cub hunting. There's something inordinately cruel about hunting immature foxes before they've had a chance to enjoy some sort of life. I've always had to remind myself all that killing is justified by the need to provide food and keep numbers down, but the poor foxes have always had my full sympathies."

Tom surprised her by asking, "What was he like?"

"Nicholas? You've never asked," she answered far too quickly. Evie shifted and set the cushion aside. She didn't expect him to justify his curiosity and a part of her didn't want him to answer because she feared he might be concerned about being in competition with a ghost. "He had a terrific sense of fun. He loved the sea. We honeymooned aboard his yacht, *Toujour Ici*, Always Here. He liked to live in the moment, which surprised me greatly when he spent so much of his time securing the future of his estates." In many ways, she thought, Tom reminded her of him. Although, Nicholas would have found her interest in detective work quite peculiar. Then again, he enjoyed losing himself in books so he might have found a way to support her interest.

Tom pushed away from the fireplace and sat opposite her. "I've been looking through the visitors book." He picked up a leather-bound book and opened it.

"Did you just change the subject?"

The edge of his lip lifted. "Belatedly, I realized I might have pressured you into talking about him. Your description of him sounded almost stilted."

Evie gave a small nod. "The first year we were married, we attended seven funerals." Evie shrugged. "Friends and family members. Nicholas would offer brief summaries full of fond memories, shared experiences and personal quirks. Almost like a commemoration... an epitaph. I think I must have picked up the habit from him." Leaning forward, she asked, "So, did you find something interesting in the visitors book?"

"Viscount Bertram was a regular visitor here." Tom held out the book.

Glancing at it, Evie frowned. "Heavens, seeing the name there brings it all back. Yes, I remember him, but only vaguely. Hunting house parties are more about the actual hunting than any sort of socializing. In fact, there were times when I was the only woman present. That's when I decided to throw myself into the sport or be left behind to occupy myself with the tedious activity of embroidery. I'd often just join the guns for luncheon and then trudge with them for the rest of the day."

He turned the page and nodded. "We can use this as a reason for calling on Lord Bertram."

"Good idea. I must admit, I haven't given much thought to strategy."

"I suppose it might be sensible to wait until we meet Alice Brown." He set the book aside. "Have you given any thought to what we're going to eat tonight? Apart from Mr. Miller I didn't see anyone else around."

"He has a cottage on the estate. His wife will bring something up. I'm sure you won't mind if we have an informal meal."

His eyebrows shot up. "Are you saying I won't have to change for dinner?"

"Shocking, isn't it. We'll even have to pour our own wine."

~

That evening...

After two days of traveling and sight-seeing, they'd both spent most of the afternoon relaxing and touring the house, something Evie decided she needed to do because she hadn't been there in so long. While Mr. Miller took care of the property, she needed to make a show of keeping an eye on things that might need fixing.

As dinner time drew closer, they set up a small table and two chairs in the drawing room. Evie refrained from mentioning the fact she and Nicholas had often enjoyed their meals in the relaxed surroundings instead of in the large dining room.

She had memories she cherished. Now, she would make new ones, even if they resembled the old ones.

Dashing down to the kitchen to get some cutlery, Evie encountered Mr. Miller coming in the back door. "We'll be dining in the drawing room, Mr. Miller. No need to fuss."

Back in the drawing room, she set the cutlery down just as Mr. Miller appeared carrying a large covered tray.

Evie gave him a cheerful smile. "Wonderful timing."

Mr. Miller cast his eyes around the room. After setting the tray down, he almost looked reluctant to leave. Finally, he said, "Mrs. Miller will surely take the broomstick to me when she finds out I've served you in the drawing room."

"Oh, I do hope she doesn't. This is perfectly fine. In fact, it's better than fine. You must thank her for us."

Shaking his head, he dug inside his pocket. "This arrived for you, milady. It's been sent from Halton House. Eddie, the local boy just dropped it off. He should've been here earlier but he came off his bicycle and had to hobble the rest of the way."

"Oh, heavens. How is he?"

"Nothing but a few scratches. Mrs. Miller is looking after him."

Evie took the letter and thanked him. Instead of opening it, she set it aside.

Mr. Miller cast his dubious eyes around one more time and, shaking his head, bid them a good night.

Pointing at the envelope, Tom asked, "Aren't you going to open it?"

"I'd rather sit down and enjoy our meal first." At a glance, she knew the letter hadn't been sent by someone from Halton House but had, in fact, been sent to Halton House before being forwarded here.

"I'm not sure I would have the patience." Tom drew out a chair for her and then sat opposite Evie.

Removing the cover, Evie and Tom were both astonished to see the variety of dishes.

"I'm almost disappointed it's not a pie. It's what I expected," he said. "Although, I would have settled for some bread and cheese."

"Mrs. Miller definitely deserves our praise." And Evie feared she might not be able to do the meal justice because, in reality, she couldn't wait to read the letter. "Let's start with the fish."

Glancing at the letter, she considered succumbing to temptation so they could discuss the contents over dinner but then Tom distracted her.

"I noticed something odd in the visitors book which led me to believe people live to unusually ripe old ages in these parts."

"Heavens, do tell."

"I noticed the same name appearing over several seasons, from year to year and throughout a long span of time. There's a Branthurst, Emerton, Rhodesdale and a few others."

Evie puzzled over it for a moment and then she smiled. "Oh, that's two generations or more. Peers sign only their surnames. It's a case of the father coming for weekends during his lifetime, and then his son inheriting the title and continuing the tradition."

"Well, that answers that. For a moment, I thought I'd discovered some sort of secret society. Then again, I'm sure if I take a closer look the writing will be slightly different." As he savored his wine, he studied her. "Do you know who the letter is from?"

Evie nodded. She managed to get through the next course before finally caving in and opening the envelope.

"Has Henrietta disowned you for abandoning her?"

"It's not from Henrietta," Evie declared as she continued reading. When she finished, she just stared at it, her lips slightly parted as she tried to digest the astonishing news.

Rather than push her for information, Tom changed the subject, "I'm intrigued to find out how you managed to keep them at Halton House. I half expected them to show up before we arrived."

She gave him a distracted smile. Turning the page, she read the last few lines again. "Heavens."

"Countess, the suspense has me on the edge of my seat."

She handed him the letter and drained her wine glass. "Do you remember me telling you I would need to make inquiries about Detective Inspector Evans?" A necessary precaution, she thought, after the inspector had shown interest in Caro. "Well, that's the answer. I contacted Detective Inspector O'Neill." It had taken the Scotland Yard detective several weeks to respond and she had almost forgotten about contacting him.

It seemed the detective had been reluctant to divulge his colleague's true identity. Evie had intended finding out if Detective Evans had any questionable or worrying habits such as drinking or gambling. Instead, she had discovered something completely unexpected.

Tom looked up. "This... This rather changes everything."

It most certainly did. Although, in what manner, she couldn't really say.

She looked down at the pudding Mrs. Miller had prepared. "I wonder if Detective Evans has told Caro?"

"I doubt it. Surely, she would have shared the news with you."

"Suddenly, I can't help seeing him in a new light. My entire perception of him has changed and now I'm worried he might not be as nice as we first thought. I know I'm jumping to conclusions, but I can't help wondering why he would keep something like this a secret."

Tom folded the letter and slipped it inside the envelope. "What will you do? Wait and see?"

Evie jumped to her feet and began pacing around the room. "He will not break Caro's heart. I will definitely see to that."

"I think you might be jumping to conclusions."

"You said it yourself. This changes everything." She

subjected the carpet to a thorough assault, pacing up and down several times. Finally, she came to a stop and gave a firm nod of her head. "Tomorrow morning, I will send Detective Evans a telegram and summon him here. That's what I am going to do. He will have to answer to me before he harms one hair on dear Caro."

CHAPTER 5

The next day
The village near the hunting lodge

"Of course, I accept full responsibility for this dreadful imbroglio," Evie fumed. "First, I put Caro in harm's way and then I thrust her into the arms of a deceitful man."

"Are you still going on about the letter?"

Evie knew she should put it all out of her mind. It should be easy enough to do since she couldn't even bring herself to talk about the contents of the missive.

"Countess, you're being hard on yourself. Caro is quite capable of making decisions and looking after herself. In any case, I'm sure there is a perfectly good explanation."

Evie checked her watch. She had sent Detective Evans a telegram half an hour ago. "He must have received it by now."

"Are you going to fret until Detective Evans arrives? Assuming he will drop everything and trek up here."

"Fret? Oh, no. I intend to fume. And he will come, if he knows what's good for him."

"You might want to get all the facts straight before you go on the warpath."

"I'm not sure I want to or need to. The facts are there. It's not often people deceive me."

Tom smiled. "I did."

"Yes, but your plan was always destined to fail because you would eventually have fallen desperately in love with me and that would have forced you to own up to the masquerade." She looked up and down the village street but didn't see any sign of someone resembling a young woman. In fact, the streets were deserted.

"I'm not sure we are in the right place." Tom mirrored her and looked up and down the small village street. "I haven't seen a single soul in over half an hour."

"Perhaps everyone is busy with their flocks of sheep or... their hunting dogs..." Evie waved her gloved hand. "Or something or other." Brightening, she added, "Maybe they're busy cleaning their guns."

Looking and sounding incredulous, Tom glanced at her. "Guns?"

Evie hid her amusement. "You must forgive me. My mind is filled with violence."

Tom chortled, "Detective Evans is beginning to gain my sympathy. I can only pray his intentions toward Caro are honest."

Caro had spent her half days and the extra time Evie had insisted she take in the detective's company and every time she'd returned from her outings, she had floated on air. Her joy had been quite contagious setting everyone off on a frenzy of exuberant excitement over the anticipated marriage proposal.

Perhaps that had been the reason for everyone's odd behavior.

The news she'd just received about Detective Evans had shaken Evie to the core. She had lived in England long enough to understand the impact of social barriers and if he thought he could flirt with Caro and then move on to someone deemed to be more suitable—

Evie tapped her foot and thought of the collection of guns at the hunting lodge.

Tom looked at his watch again. "We could at least have arranged to meet somewhere inside. The pub must have a decent fireplace."

"The Crooked Handmaiden? I'm still not sure what to make of that one."

Tom looked over his shoulder at the pub. "I'm willing to bet anything they have excellent game pies."

"Let's give Alice Brown another ten minutes."

"You said that half an hour ago."

Evie grumbled, "She might have been held up. According to Lotte Mannering, Alice Brown works at

Lynchfield Manor. Maybe she couldn't arrange to get away." Evie gasped. "Or, maybe something's happened to her."

Tom glanced around them in the way she had noticed him doing every time they were out and about. He had never ceased to be vigilant, especially when they were out in public. To this day Evie had no idea what he thought might happen.

"I doubt anyone knows me here."

It only took him a few seconds to realize what she meant. "You stand out anywhere you go, Countess."

"Are you afraid someone will snatch my handbag?"

"It's possible." He glanced down at his watch again and grimaced.

The sound of running footsteps put them on the alert. Turning, they saw a young woman hurrying toward them, her hand clutching her hat and keeping it in place.

"Do you think that's Miss Brown?" Tom asked.

"I'm not willing to place a bet on it. If I do, she might very well run right by us."

The young woman slowed down. Stopping, she swung around. With no one else about, she must have rightly assumed they were the people she had come to meet.

She walked toward them and asked, "Lady Woodridge?"

Tom nodded and stepped in front of Evie who laughed. "Do you think she might come at me with a weapon?"

"You never know."

The young woman walked the few remaining steps and nodded. "I'm Alice Brown. Lotte Mannering wrote to say you'd agreed to meet with me."

Evie introduced Tom. "Where do you suggest we go to talk?"

"The pub should be quiet enough."

"Are you sure?" Tom asked.

Alice Brown nodded. "Everyone's attending a viewing of an upcoming auction. That's why it's so quiet in the village today. I'm afraid I don't have much time."

For some reason, Tom looked less than convinced. When Evie stepped toward the pub, Tom held her back.

Ignoring his hesitation, Evie smiled. "In that case, we should go in and you can tell us what this is all about."

With Alice Brown leading the way, Evie took the opportunity to frown at Tom. "Behave yourself," she whispered. Turning to Alice, she encouraged, "Tell us about this upcoming auction."

Alice Brown nodded. "One of the local gentries is selling up and moving to London permanently. There'll be an auction of all the house contents and everyone is eager to see inside the house. The owner's sons are not interested in carrying on, in fact, they went to America soon after war broke out."

"I take it there's no title involved," Evie said.

"No. But the land has been in the family for generations."

If there had been a title, Evie thought, the eldest son would have been tied down regardless of his desire to spread his wings. Early in her marriage, she had asked Nicholas how he felt about his role and if he felt hampered by it. His casual shrug had signaled his insouciance. Then, he had gone on to explain how he had been brought up to inherit and take over the responsibility. Even if he had been thoroughly incompetent and incapable of carrying out his duty, he could have hired someone to oversee the running of the estates.

He had also stressed the fact that while duty to his family, ancestors and everyone who depended on the estate played a role in his attitude, it would never have occurred to him to walk away from something that was in his blood. In any case, he had felt lucky to have something to do as some of his contemporaries had struggled to find worthwhile pursuits and true meaning in their lives.

Tom signaled to a table as far from the main bar area as possible. Without him saying anything, Evie understood this would provide them with a modicum of privacy.

Alice Brown thanked them again for coming to see her. "I hardly know where to begin."

"Lotte said you felt there was something wrong at Lynchfield Manor," Evie prompted her.

Alice Brown shifted and glanced over her shoulder before saying, "Yes."

Evie looked at Tom and saw him studying the young woman as if trying to understand her motives for sharing this information with them.

Alice Brown clutched her handbag. For a moment, Evie thought she had changed her mind. She looked reluctant to speak and about ready to jump out of her chair and flee.

It almost surprised Evie when Alice finally spoke, her voice steady and surprisingly determined. "When war broke out, everything changed. I had only just started working at Lynchfield Manor. In fact, I'd only been there for three months before the upheaval..."

Yes, Evie thought, it had all been disruptive and everyone's lives had changed. Indeed, they all now lived in an entirely different world.

"The butler had just retired and Lord Bertram couldn't find a replacement. It was all the servants could talk about for days on end. A new butler had been engaged, but then he accepted another position closer to his family. The head footman took over but then he was called up and so another footman took over from him. Soon after, two of the remaining footmen were called up too. Some of the younger housemaids left to work in ammunition factories. The household staff kept shrinking and Lord Bertram couldn't replace them. When the cook left due to illness, he had to get a woman in from the village. He became despondent and he stopped entertaining. Before then, he would have people over all the time.

With so many sudden changes, he seemed to sink into a dark place. We often found him in the library talking to himself."

Evie sympathized, "The war had that effect on many people. The only entertainment we did during that time was to raise funds for the local hospital and for widows."

Alice shook her head. "His lordship didn't do any of that. He doesn't have a wife because she died a number of years ago. I doubt he would know the first thing about organizing such events."

"Does he have any relatives?"

"Lord Bertram was an only son and his father had been an only son. His heir is a distant cousin who visits once in a while. Nigel Bowles last visited a month ago. Lord Bertram had a sister but she never married. In any case, she died many years ago."

Alice Brown painted an unfamiliar picture. It took some doing for Evie to imagine what it would be like to have no one. Hearing of someone else's reality made her feel grateful and quite lucky to be surrounded by family and friends.

Evie imagined people who had visited Lord Bertram during happier days would have stayed away because they would have been busy with their own households and war efforts. However, there had now been ample time to recover and resume their old lifestyles. Had those years had such a tremendous impact the damage had now become irreparable?

"I take it he never quite recovered from the experience," Evie said.

"I'm not sure what happened in the latter days of the war. With my brothers gone to war, I needed to earn more to help my family so I left to work in a factory. I've only recently returned to help look after my mother and thought myself lucky to get a position at the manor house again. I don't live in so I have no idea what goes on at night. There is an estate worker, Ned Brixton, he's a head gardener. He says he's seen his lordship wandering around at night. Once, he approached him to ask if there was anything wrong and his lordship pointed a gun at him. Then, there's the stable boy. He says he's seen his lordship talking to trees."

Both Evie and Tom looked baffled enough for Alice Brown to add, "He's been seen standing in front of trees for up to half an hour."

Had old age caught up with Lord Bertram?

Seventy didn't seem to be that old.

Alice Brown continued, "After my long absence, I expected the manor house to have fallen into disrepair but it seems to be holding up well enough. The other maid, June, who only started working there after the war has been doing an amazingly good job of keeping everything tidy."

Just as Evie worried the story would unfold into a detailed description of his lordship's descent into madness, Alice Brown glanced around again and, lowering her voice, said, "Since I started working there again, I've noticed some differences. Some paintings are missing. I'm the only housemaid from before working there now and so there isn't anyone else I can ask about them."

So, the mystery involved stolen items. "What about the footman?" From what Alice Brown had said, the manor house still retained one footman.

"He went away soon after I started working at the house. He hadn't taken any time off since the war ended and he needed to visit his elderly parents. He said he would be back soon, but I suspect he might be looking for another position. So now there isn't even a footman to act as a butler. Not that anyone comes calling."

"What about the estate worker? Has he been with his lordship for long? The paintings might have been sold off before your arrival and he might have seen people coming to the house to collect them."

"Ned Brixton mostly works for the neighboring estate and that's owned by a new family. He just does odds and ends for his lordship. If he'd seen something odd, he would have mentioned it."

Evie wondered who else might have some knowledge of Lord Bertram and his activities. "What about the local doctor. Usually, they are well known to local families."

"He retired and moved away."

When the barkeeper approached them, Evie wished

they had gone to the tearooms. She didn't feel hungry, and nor did Tom.

As they all hesitated, the barkeeper suggested tea, which they agreed to.

"So, apart from his lordship's odd behavior and missing paintings, is there anything else you might have noticed?"

Alice Brown looked down at her hands and whispered, "I've had a look around for the paintings since it's quite possible he might have just moved them or put them away somewhere safe. That's when I noticed other things missing. Valuable things."

"Such as?"

"Silver cases, vases and some of the silver service."

While reluctant to suspect the servants, Evie couldn't help wondering if perhaps someone might have helped themselves to a few valuable pieces before departing from the house.

"Do you know if his accounts are honored?"

"I couldn't really say. Although, no one has complained."

Would any of the store owners complain to a housemaid? "There could be any number of reasons for valuable items going missing," Evie offered. "He might have disposed of them without anyone noticing. How large is the estate?"

"Not very large. Most of it has been sold off."

That sometimes happened as a way of covering death duties and only as a last resort. "Maybe he has debts," Evie suggested.

"I can't imagine what those would be," Alice Brown said. "I would hate to think someone is taking advantage of him. Especially as he doesn't seem to have anyone to look out for him."

Evie thought Lord Bertram should consider himself lucky to have a housemaid worrying about him.

"Does he ever leave the estate?"

"No. It's almost as if he's given up."

"What about his heir?" Tom asked.

"That would be Nigel Bowles. I'm afraid I don't know much about him except that he was a captain in the war. As I said, I haven't been back long, so I can't really say if he has been visiting more regularly than the times I've seen him."

Evie glanced at Tom. "That's something we could easily follow up on, I'm sure." They could at least try to locate him and make contact. "It's very kind of you to be concerned."

"I'm just ever so grateful to be able to get some sort of employment and still be able to look after my mother. Lord Bertram has always been fair and not at all demanding."

Did she fear losing her position?

Almost as if reading her mind, Alice Brown said, "I know what this must sound like. I'm poking my nose where it doesn't belong and all for a self-serving purpose. Yes, I do need the job, but I am also truly concerned for his lordship."

"You are to be commended. I hope his lordship recognizes what a treasure you are."

Thinking of the housemaid's conscientious efforts, Evie felt a sudden pang of guilt over her harsh and unfair treatment of Caro and Millicent as well as the other servants. Of course, Tom would say she was merely being hard on herself.

"You said you don't live there so there's no way of knowing if he receives visitors at night."

"Yes, that's right, but if he had callers, there would be some evidence the next morning, such as glasses or cups. But I've never seen anything to suggest he had been entertaining."

Before the tea even arrived, Alice Brown shot to her feet. "I've stayed away too long. I should head back now." She gave them an apologetic smile.

Evie dug around inside her handbag. Finding a piece of paper, she wrote down the address for the hunting lodge as well as the telephone number. "Do let us know if anything else crops up."

Alice took the piece of paper. "I hope you can find some way of looking into this."

Evie watched the young housemaid dash out of the pub. "Well, Mr. Winchester, it looks like we have a mystery to unravel."

"A well-staged mystery?"

"What do you mean?" Evie asked.

"It seems everyone we might have suspected of carting off the silver is either no longer employed by his lordship or no longer visits."

"That's interesting that you should try to point the finger of suspicion at others," Evie mused. "I'm inclined to look no further than Viscount Bertram."

"You suspect him of stealing his own possessions?"

"I've come to accept the fact that we live in a strange world full of strange occurrences."

CHAPTER 6

First port of call

With the entire pub to themselves, Tom and Evie sat back to mull over everything Alice Brown had told them.

Evie studied the bottom of her teacup. "I'm struck by the fact she didn't simply come straight out and say there were paintings and other items missing." While the young housemaid had been pressed for time, eager to return, and concerned about being overheard, she had provided them with a great deal of information.

"Yes," Tom nodded. "Instead of cutting to the chase, she gave us a methodical account."

"Are you still suspicious of her? You certainly looked it from the first moment she appeared."

Tom shrugged. "I'm merely getting into the spirit of the game."

"Suspect everyone? Yes, you have a point. However, if we are to believe her story, we don't seem to have many people to suspect." With no apparent visitors and no outings made by his lordship, they clearly had their work cut out for them. "On the other hand, I'm thinking there might be a reason why she gave us such a detailed account. She must have had plenty of time to think about it. Seeking outside help can't have been a decision made lightly since it would involve inviting strangers to intrude on his lordship's private life." And, Evie thought, if his lordship questioned the presence of unexpected guests poking around, he would only have a couple of people to suspect—the housemaids.

They both looked out the window but found nothing to distract them as the village remained devoid of people.

"I think it might be a good idea to wander around," she suggested. "At least we know where everyone is. And, with any luck, we might be in time to see the auction items."

"Are you actually interested in acquiring more bits and pieces for your massive collection?"

"Not really. Although, one never knows what one might find. I've never been to an auction of household curios."

After finishing their tea, Evie and Tom approached the barkeeper and asked about the house inspection.

They were directed to a manor house on the outskirts of the village.

During the short drive there, Evie fidgeted with her handbag and tried to stop herself from looking at the time. She knew Detective Evans would provide an explanation in due course. Regardless, she felt defenseless and quite unable to fight off the feeling of anxiety sweeping through her. The news she had received involved Caro and the outcome, if it didn't go her maid's way, would affect her for years to come.

Belatedly, Evie wished she hadn't meddled. She knew she had set something in motion and she also admitted she had been highly presumptuous in thinking it was her place to interfere.

"But it is," she murmured.

Caro didn't just work for her, she was part of her world, Evie thought as she turned her attention to the scenic countryside.

Leaving behind the small village with its vicarage, schoolhouse and surrounding manor houses, they had driven past several farmhouses with cowsheds, barns and cottages. Slowing down several times to give way to livestock and other vehicles including several carts and horses, they realized not everyone had rushed to view the contents coming up for sale.

But enough people had made a pilgrimage to the house.

They came across some motor cars pulled up by the side of the narrow country lane they had turned into.

The line of motors stretched for some distance and straight up to the gated entrance to the manor house.

Tom drove on a bit and managed to wedge the roadster between two other motor cars.

Laughing, he said, "If worse comes to worst, we can cut across the field."

There were people milling about the gardens inspecting the rose bushes. "You don't suppose those are being sold too? How dreadful."

Two columns marked the entrance to the house and they had to sidestep a couple of people who appeared to be hesitating. They were dressed in their Sunday best and were most likely only interested in seeing how the other half lived.

Evie smiled at one couple who looked young enough to be considered newlyweds. The husband nudged the wife who in turn tugged him away. Evie widened her smile and threw in a nod of encouragement to which they responded by taking a few tentative steps inside the house.

Walking in, Evie saw chairs had been arranged in the main hall with a lectern at the end where, no doubt, the auctioneer would stand.

"It looks like the auction is actually taking place today," Tom said. "And it seems absolutely everything is up for sale."

When she drew him away from the main hall saying they should look at the rest on offer, Tom looked surprised. "Don't tell me you're suddenly keen to pick up a bargain."

"Heavens, no. I just realized this is a wonderful opportunity. Everyone who lives in the area is here."

"You want to catalogue them for future reference?"

Evie cringed. "Does it make me sound absolutely grisly in a distasteful sort of way?"

"Oh, Countess. No. Never."

"Mr. Winchester, you tease me." Brightening, she nudged him. "I'm going to take a wild guess and say they are the owners." She signaled toward a corner of the drawing room they had walked into.

A couple stood by the window. They looked old enough to have grown-up children. At first glance, their expressions looked blank. However, after a moment, Evie decided they displayed a mixture of bewilderment and dismay but only because she imagined being in their place and feeling baffled by having so many people traipsing through her house eager to acquire a bargain. "I doubt I would be able to stand it."

"What?" Tom asked.

"Parting with something that has been cherished. I don't mean to put things above people or experiences. However, objects form a part of the backdrop of life. I'm not sure I would have the courage to hover around and watch it all disintegrate right before my eyes."

"They do look uncomfortable," Tom observed.

Evie wondered if they should approach them. And say what? *I'm sorry for your loss?*

According to Alice Brown, they had a house in town so they weren't exactly headed for the poorhouse.

The shuffling of feet and the scraping of chairs took

their attention back to the hall. Everyone in the drawing room, including the owners, moved toward the door.

"The auction is about to start."

The supposed owners walked ahead of them and went to stand in a corner while Evie and Tom sat on the first chairs available.

The auctioneer cleared his throat and gave brief instructions on how the auction would proceed.

Tom leaned toward Evie and whispered, "Whatever you do, don't nod or raise your hand. There's only so much room in the roadster."

Smiling, she glanced away and her attention fell on a painting of a horse which, even to her untrained eye, looked very much like a *Stubbs*; the English painter known for his pictures of horses. Quite valuable, she thought. As it did not have a number she assumed the owners would not be parting with the piece.

A succession of items appeared, brought up to the front and displayed for everyone to see; silver candlesticks and vases, chairs and side tables. In all instances, the bidding began slow and cautious with the auctioneer issuing warnings that no such pieces could be had anywhere for so little.

Evie could not recall a single instance in her life when she'd had to purchase a piece of furniture. Halton House had already been furnished by previous generations and there was no need to add new pieces or exchange old for new. It simply wasn't done.

However, if she had to furnish a new house, she

would have tried her best to outbid everyone as she found all the pieces charming.

When a high-backed chair came up, she thought of the village school teacher back home who lived in a small cottage near the school house. Evie had visited her not long ago and had found her cottage furnished with only a few pieces. At the time she'd thought that had been a personal preference. Now, she wondered if the schoolteacher might appreciate a new... old chair.

Almost as if he'd read her intentions, Tom rested his hand on hers and frowned at Evie.

"What?" she mouthed.

"Don't," he mouthed back.

Smiling at him, she spent the next few minutes thinking they would have a lot of reminiscences to share in their old age.

With each fall of the auctioneer's hammer, the owners appeared to shrink inside themselves and look more downcast.

Evie prayed for them to see past their material loss.

At that moment, she felt quite ill at ease with being a silent witness to their obvious despair. She imagined the way they appeared to feel had nothing to do with the sale of furniture. Rather, she thought they were coming to grips with the unavoidable fact that their children's lives were elsewhere and the future they had envisioned of close family ties would never be realized.

Murmurs of appreciation rose around her. Looking back toward the auctioneer, she saw a new item had been brought up.

Not the Stubbs painting, as she would have expected by the obvious interest. Instead, the auctioneer's assistant held up a photograph of a horse while the auctioneer made a joke about the awkwardness of bringing the horse inside.

Evie turned and saw the owner looking down and shaking his head.

To Evie's surprise, Tom had shifted and now sat on the edge of his chair.

"Don't you dare," she whispered. "If I can't buy something then neither can you."

"But it placed at the Grand National."

Evie gave him a censorious lift of her eyebrow. "Can't you see they are heartbroken over losing their possessions?"

He looked determined and eager to argue the point. Instead, with the reluctance and petulance of a boy deprived of a toy, Tom sat back and crossed his arms over his chest.

Despite the obvious enthusiasm from everyone present, the auctioneer had trouble engaging anyone's interest in a starting bid. It seemed few people could afford to buy the racehorse. She realized this could be because it would take a lot of money to keep and train the horse.

As the auctioneer continued his efforts, baiting those present with the horse's pedigree, Evie wondered why the owners had put the horse up for sale in this manner. If she wanted to sell any of her livestock, she would engage an agent to take care of it. Why hadn't the owners organized the sale of the horse through *Tattersalls*, the place to buy and sell horses?

"The Guildfords must have hit rock bottom," someone behind Evie murmured.

Evie glanced at the couple she could now identify by name. Mrs. Guildford lifted her chin and looked defiant and determined while Mr. Guildford continued to look down at the floor.

Lost in her thoughts, she became vaguely aware of something the auctioneer said about taking any bids. That's when someone two rows up from Evie raised their hand.

"It's going for next to nothing," Tom muttered and glanced at Evie.

"We already have horses and rarely ride. What do you want with a racing horse?"

He opened his mouth to reply only to shrug and say, "But it's going for a pittance."

"So, you just want the bargain."

"Wouldn't you?"

"I don't know because you've placed an embargo on me bidding on anything."

"I suppose we could compromise. You could maybe... purchase a little something..."

Evie wanted to tell him she didn't necessarily need his permission. "Are you saying I should settle for something small while you get the big horse? Where is the fairness in that?"

"Is this about size?" he asked, his tone sounding defensive.

Fully engaged in their murmured exchange they missed the hammer going down.

The horse sold for an amount too great for an average person but quite insignificant for anyone of means.

Evie had no trouble identifying the winner of the bid. The man stood erect, with his chest puffed out and his eyes brimming with a look of cruel triumph.

When Tom spent the following ten minutes avoiding her gaze, Evie suspected he might be giving her the silent treatment. She didn't take his reaction to heart. Knowing him, he merely wanted to make a game of it.

After seeing so many items coming up for sale and not learning anything of particular interest about the people attending, Evie wanted to leave but thought that might send a negative message to everyone else and especially to the owners who, despite the mixture of distress and sadness they displayed, were probably hoping to sell every last item. So Evie bided her time.

At last, the auction ended and they made their way out of the house and walked in silence toward the roadster.

Giving Tom an impish smile, she said, "I suppose I should apologize. That horse might have gone on to win the Grand National."

"Are you trying to make me cry?" he asked.

"To be fair, you're the one who started it. And I'm not sure what you have against ornaments."

"There seem to be an awful lot of them at Halton

House and I'm constantly having to take care I don't topple something over."

"The unwritten rule being that if you break something, you'll have to pay for it?" she teased.

Tom studied her for a long moment and then sighed. "If you must know..." he seemed to change his mind.

"What?"

"I bet you walked into Halton House and felt right at home straightaway."

She had. "And you didn't?"

"Sometimes, I think the servants feel more at home there than I do. In fact, there are times when I feel like a veritable bull in a china shop."

"I never knew this about you. What else are you hiding from me?"

He opened the passenger door for her, his expression grim.

As Evie settled in, she gave him a worried look only to frown when she saw him smiling.

Evie gaped at him. "Did you just deceive me again?" Belatedly, she realized she'd never seen him looking uncomfortable at Halton House. For a moment, she had even begun to worry he might want them to move.

He settled in the driver's seat and smiled at her. "Seriously, did you really want to buy any of those bits and bobs?"

No, not really. "Only if I felt it would help the owners but they looked too heartbroken and the item would forever be associated with that."

They had to wait for the other drivers to move their motor cars and finally they made their way back to the hunting lodge.

Evie didn't pay any attention to the scenery. Instead, she kept her thoughts occupied with the sale of the horse.

With no one to inherit the house and land, the Guildford couple were losing a source of income, but they would have the proceeds from the sale which they could invest. However, selling the racehorse didn't make sense. Horses could be stabled. In fact, most owners tended to do that.

What on earth had compelled them to sell it?

CHAPTER 7

Best laid plans

*E*vie pushed all thoughts about the sale of the racehorse out of her mind and sat back to enjoy the pretty countryside and woods. When the lodge came into view, she looked for signs of activity around the Queen Anne box shaped house.

The first to arrive would be the housemaids to open the rooms, along with the kitchen servants to prepare for the arrival of the storm. And she had no doubt there would be one.

Taking the reins, she had set out to manage her household in an impersonal manner. However, judging by the guilt she felt, her actions certainly didn't suit her personality. If only she'd been able to think of some other course of action that would achieve the desired result of pacifying everyone.

She still hoped everyone would simply take a step back and just calm down. She hadn't enjoyed the strongarm tactics she'd employed and she had no idea if her experiment would work. Luckily, Tom hadn't questioned her strange method. If he had, she would have struggled to explain it.

Heavens! *What had she done?*

With several days to think about the treatment Evie had subjected her to, Henrietta's opinions would have simmered to a boiling point. Evie expected the dowager would have a great deal to say about her cruel treatment and Evie was sure that's how she would refer to it.

Mr. Miller emerged from the side of the house, a walking stick in hand, not that he needed the assistance. An agile man with a rugged looking face, he used the stick as an extension of his hand to poke at things or point.

As Evie descended from the roadster, he tipped his hat as a greeting and rested both hands on the stick handle.

"Mr. Miller, has anyone arrived yet?" Evie asked.

Mr. Miller's nod served as an economical response. Evie tried to read his expression but failed miserably. Now that the kitchen servants had arrived, would Mrs. Miller feel slighted and would she take out her objections by chasing poor Mr. Miller with her broomstick?

"The housemaids are busy preparing the rooms,

milady. I've just unloaded the produce brought up from Halton House and the kitchen is a hive of activity."

Evie listened with rapt attention. She'd never heard him speak at such great length about any subject. Before he could clam up, Evie asked him if he knew anything about Lord Bertram.

Mr. Miller looked down at the ground as if gathering his thoughts. When he looked up, he said, "An odd fellow, deeply disturbed by the war. That's what everyone in the district says."

"Do you know if he receives any visitors?"

Mr. Miller settled his walking stick on the crook of his arm and struck up a pensive pose. "If he does it would be in the dead of night. Ned Brixton might be able to help you with more information."

Evie remembered Alice Brown mentioning the head gardener who actually worked in the neighboring property.

She glanced at Tom to see if he had any questions he wanted to ask only to remember the telegram she had sent. "Have we received any letters or telegrams?"

"No, milady."

Thanking him, they headed toward the front entrance. Just as they were about to enter, Mr. Miller called out, "By the way, your chauffeur also arrived a half hour ago."

Evie had asked Edmonds to drive up so the dowagers and Toodles would have access to a motor car. "Ask him to come in and see us in the drawing room, please."

Tom helped her out of her coat. "I'm suddenly feeling ravenously hungry."

Evie nodded in agreement. "It might be a good idea to fortify ourselves before everyone else arrives. If you must know, I've entertained a few regrets."

"I'm sure Edmonds will be able to set you at ease. He's bound to have news about everyone's reactions to your firm yet underhanded tactics."

"I see, you are poking fun at me."

"I'm sure I wouldn't dare. You might send me a letter too and put me firmly in my place." When she didn't reply, he chuckled. "Countess, I'm trying to prepare you for their imminent arrival. You'll have to think on your feet."

"Yes, I'm afraid you might be right. But we should wait to hear what Edmonds has to say." She turned and walked into the drawing room, saying, "Will you ever tire of teasing me?"

"I doubt I ever will."

She hoped he wouldn't because she rather enjoyed it. "I'd kill for a cup of tea but I don't want to make a fuss. Everyone must be so busy."

Tom laughed. "You really aren't much of a countess." Picking up the visitors book, he settled down by the fireplace to have a look through it.

"I'm guessing you're looking to see if the Guildfords have been here."

He nodded. "I don't see their name so I suppose they are not gentrified enough."

"Nonsense. We used to welcome anyone who

wished to shoot or hunt. In fact, Mr. Miller will confirm it. His daughter learned to ride here and she's an excellent shot."

The door opened and Edmonds walked in. To their surprise, he carried a tray. Setting it down on a small table, he stood back. "We thought you might like some tea, my lady."

"How perfectly wonderful. Thank you, Edmonds." As she poured the tea, she asked, "What news do you bring?"

"News?"

"Yes, I wish to hear about everyone back home. I've been worried about the dowagers and Toodles."

Edmonds stood with his hands behind his back and stared into space.

Reading his silence as reluctance, Evie encouraged, "Don't leave anything out, Edmonds."

"Well... the day after you left, I drove Toodles to the dower house and a short while later she asked me to drive her back to Halton House and to be ready to drive her on to the train station."

Surprised, Evie looked up. "She's here?"

"No, my lady, she's not."

Seeing the chauffeur's hesitation, Evie tried to remain calm but she prepared for the worst. Handing the cup to Tom, she picked up her own cup and sat back.

"So... you drove her to the train station," she mused. "Did she get off alright?" And, she thought, in which direction had she headed?

"Not exactly, my lady." Edmonds closed his eyes almost as if pained by something. "While Toodles went in to organize her luggage, I walked down to the stables and when I returned I found the motor had a flat tire. It had actually been punctured."

"Heavens." Evie exchanged a look of surprise with Tom. "How did that happen?"

Edmonds shrugged. "I couldn't really say, my lady. I'd been gone for no longer than ten minutes. Anyhow, just as I found the punctured tire, Toodles came out followed by several footmen carrying her luggage. You see... she wished to go to town."

"Did she?" Had that been Toodles' reaction to the letter she'd sent her?

"She was most determined and she looked none too pleased about the delay. So I rolled up my sleeves and changed the tire."

"What did Toodles do in the meantime?"

"She... She huffed and puffed. And she muttered a great deal."

"What about?"

Edmonds hesitated. Finally, he said, "Something about overstaying her welcome."

Evie's cup rattled on its saucer. "Heavens. Where did she get that idea from?"

"I don't like to say, my lady."

"Please do. On second thought, you don't have to." Edmonds had said her granny had stayed at the dower house for only a short while. Had there been a disagreement?

Looking up, she met Tom's steady gaze.

"So what happened next?" Tom asked.

"Once I had the punctured tire replaced and the luggage loaded, we headed out." Edmonds stopped and took a deep swallow. "We made it as far as the gates. They were padlocked."

Evie's eyebrows hitched up. What? Who? Why? She couldn't form the words to ask.

"And we couldn't find the caretaker and I couldn't access his cottage because the door was locked so I had to drive back to get cutters for the padlock." Edmonds stopped again and appeared to be reluctant to reveal the rest.

"Have we heard the worst?" Evie asked.

Edmonds sighed. "I found something to cut the padlock and chain... but..." he drew in a deep breath.

Evie braced herself.

"In the time that it took us to drive to the stables and back again, a cart and horse had pulled up outside the gates."

"Outside the gates?"

Edmonds' eyes bounced around the drawing room, almost as if he couldn't quite bring himself to look at her. "Right outside the gates, my lady."

"You mean, the cart blocked the way?"

He nodded. "That's correct. Also... One of the wheels had come off. Coincidentally, Lady Henrietta's butler, Bradley, happened to be there. He'd driven up and..." Edmonds' cheeks colored. "Well... his motor car had broken down outside the gates." Edmonds fell silent and looked almost relieved to have finally finished his tale.

Evie leaned forward and set her cup of tea down. After a moment of deliberation, she found her voice. "I take it you didn't get to the train station."

Edmonds shook his head. "By the time I cut through the chain, moved the cart and helped Bradley get the motor started, we knew Toodles had missed the train."

"I see." She didn't really. "When did all this happen?" she asked. Although, she already knew the answer.

"Two days ago, my lady. I left early the next day to drive up here... as instructed."

As instructed by her letter, Evie thought. "And Toodles? Whatever happened to my granny?"

"She remained at Halton House."

"How do you know. Didn't you just say you left early the next day?"

He gave a stiff nod and lifted his gaze up to the ceiling.

Evie groaned under her breath. "Good heavens. There's more. I just know there is more."

"I'm afraid so, my lady. Half way up here, I stopped for the night at a pub." Edmonds shifted and then he delivered the information as if trying to get it over and done with. "I placed a telephone call to Halton House. I spoke with Caro and she informed me Toodles had been locked up in her room and they were frantically trying to find the key to her room."

Evie's voice hitched. "What?"

"After missing her train, Toodles had an early dinner and retired to her room. The next morning, she slept in. When one of the maids took her breakfast up, she found the door locked. Caro had no idea how it had all happened. When I telephoned, they had been at it for several hours. In fact, for most of the day. Because of the delay in opening the door, they managed to get some food to her by lowering a basket from the room above hers. So, she had breakfast and lunch in her room and, as they still hadn't found the key, they were about to serve her some dinner."

Overcoming her disbelief, Evie asked, "Do you think it's safe to assume someone wanted to keep Toodles at Halton House?"

"I believe so, my lady."

"And I suppose this has something to do with her brief visit to the dower house." Evie huffed out a breath and looked at Tom, her voice filled with disbelief. "What do you make of all this?"

"I'm not sure but I suspect Henrietta might be at the heart of it all."

"What do you think the chances are they will ever make it up here?"

Tom leaned forward. "Well, if you piece it all together, I think we can assume Henrietta wished to stop Toodles from leaving. I'm willing to bet she will do all she can to bring Toodles up here."

Evie thanked Edmonds. Sitting back, she stared at the fireplace. "We should do our best to enjoy tonight. I believe it might be our last night of peace and quiet for some time."

"I've heard say madness runs in the family," Tom murmured, "but you should be fine because you're not related to Henrietta by blood."

"No, but I am related to Toodles."

CHAPTER 8

The next day

$\mathcal{E}$vie woke up to a misty morning and a foggy head. She remembered stirring from her comfortable chair at the stroke of midnight and declaring she would abandon all attempts to understand what had happened at Halton House until the next day.

Her brow furrowed. "Well, today is the next day and I'm still perplexed." All might be revealed when the others joined them at the hunting lodge or they might decide to spare her the details and pretend nothing had happened.

Had her absence had the opposite desired effect and brought them all undone?

Evie wanted to trust them and to believe they could

sort out their own problems, whatever they might be, but she had trouble erasing the image of the three of them—Henrietta, Sara and Toodles—engaging in a verbal skirmish, scoring hits, purging themselves of everything they had kept under wraps, spurring each other on...

Evie raked her fingers through her hair. "Good heavens." Had Toodles been rescued from her locked room? Had she argued with Henrietta and had she intended going to town or had she meant to trek back to America?

Evie's mind filled with a barrage of questions.

Tempted to throw the covers over her head, Evie forced herself to jump out of bed and prepare to face the day ahead.

She had been managing without anyone's assistance for several days now but that would soon end with Caro's arrival.

"Not entirely without help," Evie said as she removed a label pinned to her skirt. Caro had gone to the trouble of matching everything for her and someone had contradicted her choices. Frowning, Evie tried to make sense of the word that had been crossed out and replaced with an alternative message.

It seemed Millicent thought her brown skirt would go better with the pale green blouse which she would find in the small suitcase. Evie glanced at the pink blouse Caro had selected. Pink. Green. It made no difference to her.

Once she finished dressing, she made her way down

to the dining room where she found Tom already enjoying his breakfast.

Hearing her come in, he asked, "Are we all set to tackle our mystery?" When he glanced up from his breakfast, he dug inside his pocket and drew out a small piece of paper. After reading it, he looked at her and his eyebrows lifted.

Noticing this, she asked, "What?"

"Is that skirt really meant to go with that blouse?"

"What do you mean?"

He looked at her with a straight face but it didn't last. A moment passed and he burst into laughter. "My apologies, Countess. This morning, I found a note in my luggage saying I should comment on your clothes. There's a list with dates and corresponding clothes. From memory, you've been wearing the correct ensembles. Today, however, you seem to have mixed something up."

Evie groaned under her breath. "I'm trying not to think what will happen when Caro and Millicent finally arrive. I only hope they have worked out their differences." She sat down opposite him and studied the dishes on offer. "We must find a way to see Lord Bertram today. My head's been filled with too many irrelevant thoughts so I'm afraid I haven't come up with any ideas. Have you?"

He took a leisurely sip of his coffee and nodded. "I thought we might drive up to Lynchfield Manor and knock on the front door."

"I can't believe you said that with a straight face.

However, that might actually work, but what then? How do we justify our impromptu visit?"

He raised his cup in a salute. "We then rely on the art of improvisation."

"You want to make it all up as we go? But that means paying attention to what we each say and, worse, actually remembering the details."

"I doubt we'll have any trouble. By the sounds of it, Lord Bertram is not quite right." He tapped his head with his finger.

"That's an unfair appraisal of a man we haven't even met yet." She looked around the table. "I suppose there isn't any mail."

"Detective Inspector Evans might be calling your bluff. Either that, or he's not used to receiving a snappy summons from a peer." Tom looked up in thought. "Or should that be peeress?"

"Yes, and my telegram was not snappy. Perhaps a touch monosyllabic. Maybe even brief, but certainly not curt." She gave him a worried look. "Surely not."

Tom laughed. "You are so easy to bait."

"Did I happen to mention I am a fine shot?"

Later that day...

Evie and Tom spent the morning continuing their inspection of the hunting lodge and the rest of the estate while they tried to think of a way to meet Lord Bertram without letting him know they were investigating him. As Tom seemed to be more interested in becoming acquainted with the estate, Evie did most of the talking.

The hunting lodge had a fine stable of horses all going to waste. It seemed such a shame to have stayed away all this time but Mr. Miller assured Evie there had been plenty of people more than happy to take the horses out for rides.

It suddenly occurred to Evie they could turn this into a productive venture. With the war over, there were masses of visitors to England eager to capture the essence of country living and not everyone knew someone who owned a country house. She mentioned this to Mr. Miller who seemed rather taken with the idea. Of course, once Seth grew up he would want to use the hunting lodge and revive the tradition she had allowed to lapse but there was quite a long time before that happened.

She answered Tom's surprise by saying, "People pay to have a look around grand houses and stay in hotels. Whatever we do will only be temporary. Unless, of course, you wish to take up regular hunting."

His blank expression said it all. However, he added, "I hope you're not thinking of doing that at Halton House."

Evie brightened. "What a wonderful idea. Instead of

a fête to raise funds for the local hospital, we could open the house to the public."

They talked about it while they sat down to enjoy a mid-morning cup of tea, after which, they made their way to Lynchfield Manor.

"Even if all those ideas come to nothing, I managed to take my mind off Detective Evans and everyone else. Although, along the way, we seem to have forgotten to come up with a solid plan. We can't simply burst in on Lord Bertram."

Coming up to the village, Tom stopped and looked at her. "Your voice still sounds quivery."

"I hadn't noticed."

"It's been like that since breakfast. Are you going to hold your ground or cave in to Henrietta's whims?"

"I have no idea what you're talking about."

"Countess, you're too soft." He chortled. "If you're going to take the reins, I'm afraid you'll have to crack the whip."

Evie grumbled under her breath. "Do you think everyone's odd behavior is due to the element of excitement I've introduced?"

After giving it some thought, he nodded. "That hadn't occurred to me but you might be right."

"If that's the case, then they are all suffering from disappointment because the last few weeks have been rather mundane."

"You mean, apart from everyone's odd behavior."

"Yes. I fear they might expect me to provide them

with entertainment on a daily basis." Looking around the village, she said, "Why did you stop here?"

He pointed toward a woman wearing a checkered coat in bright orange and brown and a floppy velvet beret with a pheasant feather waving in the light breeze.

"Are you trying to draw my attention to her hat?" she asked and adjusted her own floppy velvet beret with a pheasant feather.

"Look at the basket she's carrying."

"It looks heavy. Perhaps you should assist her."

"Yes, that's what I was thinking."

Tom hopped out of the roadster and approached the woman who was about to walk into the pub.

He blocked her view so Evie couldn't see the woman's expression or reaction to being accosted on the street.

After a short exchange, Tom held the pub door open for her. She walked in and Tom hurried back, his hand clutching his chest.

"Good heavens. What's wrong with you?" she asked.

"I found a solution to our problem."

"Which problem?" They had acquired several.

Tom settled down in the driver's seat and, still clutching his chest, he looked ahead and smiled. "I must admit, it is a brilliant idea."

"I can't agree with you until you tell me what it is."

Laughing under his breath, Tom leaned in.

Distracted by his gaze and his soft laughter, Evie didn't notice him digging inside his coat. Suddenly, something wet brushed against her chin. Evie yelped. "Good heavens." An adorable little head popped up right in front of her. "What on earth? Hello. What do we have here?" She wrapped her hands around the little puppy and gazed into his big brown eyes.

"It's a French Bulldog," Tom said.

"You got me a dog?"

"I took advantage of an opportunity. He's going to act as our prop and help us get inside Lord Bertram's house."

Evie looked at the puppy. "Was that woman selling it?"

"She was meeting us. This morning I asked Mr. Miller if he knew of anyone selling puppies. He'd heard of this woman who'd been trying to find homes for her litter and she had one left. I contacted her and arranged for us to meet her here."

Evie tucked the puppy under her chin. "So, I get to keep him?"

He shrugged. "A while back you said you wanted a dog."

Yes, but she'd been thinking about getting a Labrador.

"He's perfect," Tom declared. "A dog his size can easily travel with us."

"So how does he fit into this master plan you have worked out all by yourself? The one I've yet to hear about."

"I told you. We walk up to the main door and knock. Actually, you walk up and I hide somewhere out of sight with this little guy." He told her the rest of the plan.

Looking puzzled, she asked, "So which idea came first? The puppy or the rest?"

He scratched the puppy's head. "One thing led to another and then it all fell into place. At least, I hope it will."

It seemed they were going to a lot of trouble to find out if Lord Bertram had been selling off his paintings.

"I suppose we must think of a name for him."

"Holmes?"

CHAPTER 9

A game of subterfuge

Lynchfield Manor

They found Lynchfield Manor located a short distance from the village. Surrounded by a pretty park with a back drop of the hills beyond, the only sign of life they saw were a few birds flitting about.

The three storey rectangular house, constructed of silver-white stone and probably built in the eighteenth-century, surprised Evie. Although modest in size, certainly if compared to Halton House, it looked rather large for one person. Evie hoped Lord Bertram's heir had a large family. Wincing, she realized she'd been feeling uneasy about Lord Bertram cutting himself off from the world. She knew she viewed his circumstances from her own experience. There were quite a few residents in the village of Halton who lived alone but they were included in village life and visited by concerned parishioners, including herself.

Evie looked down at the puppy and considered changing his name to Henry. "He doesn't look like a Holmes."

"He'll grow into it. Won't you Holmes?" Tom laughed. "See, he's already responding to the name."

"Henry." The puppy ignored her. "Henry," she tried again and again, but every time the puppy ignored her. "Fine, Holmes it is." The puppy squirmed and settled under her chin. "I'm not sure your plan will work. What if Lord Bertram asks what we're doing driving out this way?"

"We'll say we're visiting the area and got lost."

"And how did I lose Holmes?"

"He just jumped out of your arms."

Evie gaped at him. "You're not afraid we'll come across as absent-minded or, worse, feeble-minded, losing one thing after another?"

"Once we gain entry you can dissuade Lord Bertram of that belief by delighting him with your bright intellect. Can you recite poetry?"

"Even if I could, how would I work it into the conversation? Especially after losing Holmes. I'm sure I should be frantic with worry and concerned he'll never turn up again. Am I to use poetry as a soothing balm for my nerves?"

Laughing, he brought the roadster to a stop. "Hand him over."

Holmes whimpered. "I don't think he likes the idea of being used as a prop or of being handed over to you. At least with me he knows what to expect. A poetry reciting, raving mad Countess."

"Well, he'll have to learn to step up to the plate." Taking the puppy, Tom climbed out of the roadster and disappeared around the side of the house.

Adjusting the collar on her coat, Evie walked up to the front door and pulled the bell. Stepping back, she looked up at the windows and wondered if Alice Brown would answer the door. After a few moments, she thought she heard someone bellow. Then, after what seemed like an eternity, the door opened.

Lord Bertram, she presumed.

Dressed in mismatched clothes, his red velvet coat appeared to have been thrown on at the last minute while his blue trousers were held in place by a bright yellow necktie. His strange attire was completed by a pair of work boots.

He stood looking at her, his sharp blue eyes glowering at Evie, his thumb hitched on his pocket while his fingers tapped with impatience.

He raked his fingers through his thick mop of white hair and cleared his throat. Without preamble, he launched into an explanation, one which suggested he'd been in the middle of a thought, "It's the pigs, you see. I've been feeding them because no one else seems capable of doing it. Not that I would want them to." He appeared to remember himself and straightened. "And who might you be?"

Evie introduced herself using her real name. Belatedly, she wondered if she should have made one up. In further hindsight, she wished she had a readymade list of aliases to fall back on, something she would clearly need to work on.

"Lady Woodridge? I knew a Lady Woodridge once but you look nothing like her. What seems to be the problem? I assume there is one because I can't imagine why you would call on me."

"My apologies for disturbing you." As he hadn't introduced himself, she had no idea how to address him. "I seem to have lost my dog and I feared you might be distraught to find people wandering around your property. You see, Holmes ran off and disappeared around the building and my friend went searching for him."

Before he could respond, someone called out, "Is there something the matter, Bertram?"

"Lady Woodridge has lost her dog," Lord Bertram replied at the top of his voice.

Evie saw a man approaching the front door. "Perhaps we should assist her ladyship."

When the man reached the front door, Evie immediately recognized him. He had been the winning bidder for the racehorse at the auction.

"Well, aren't you going to introduce us?" he asked.

Lord Bertram frowned. "She says she's Lady Woodridge, but she looks nothing like her."

"So, you've met her ladyship."

"Not this one." Lord Bertram frowned. "Or maybe I have. I just don't happen to remember right this minute."

The man smiled at Evie. "You must forgive Lord Bertram, he's been feeding his pigs and they always leave him in a strange mood. I'm Mr. Roland Carter and this is Viscount Bertram."

"How d'you do."

"Perhaps you should invite her ladyship in, Bertram, and we can sort out this business of the dog."

"He won't be in the house," Lord Bertram declared. "Not unless I left the back door open. Yes, yes. You should come in. Is the dog rabid?"

"Heavens, no, he's quite placid." Evie walked in and sent her gaze around the hall to take in its white walls covered with paintings, shields and swords.

"I'll ring for some tea. Although, heaven knows if that girl, Alice, will answer since she obviously didn't hear the doorbell. We'll go through to the library." He headed in one direction only to change his mind and turn toward another door.

Evie followed Lord Bertram and as they were about to enter the library, she turned to Mr. Carter. "Are you an old friend of the family?"

"Oh, yes. Bertram and I go back a long way."

Mr. Carter looked to be in his fifties while his lordship had to be facing his late seventies. How had they befriended each other? Where had they met? At a social occasion? His lordship had only become a recluse after the war. If they went back a long way, had they met regularly?

Without being prompted, Mr. Carter explained, "He and my father were friends."

Evie wondered if she had appeared to be overly curious. Had she given herself away with an unconscious lift of the eyebrow? Such reactions, she knew, had to be curtailed. Heavens, she would have to study herself in the mirror. As a lady detective, she would need to be in full control of her facial expressions and not give away her thoughts.

Lord Bertram cleared some books from a wingback chair. "You must excuse the state of this room. Nothing is where it's supposed to be so I'm trying to reorganize it all."

Books were stacked on every available surface. There were also some paintings stacked against the wall, which must have been brought in from another room because she didn't see where they could possibly have been hung since all the wall spaces were taken up with bookcases.

"Lord Bertram is trying to find a system that works for him but he can't decide if the books should be shelved by order of title, author or subject matter," Mr. Carter explained.

"Which one usually comes to mind?" Evie asked.

Lord Bertram raised a finger. "Aha! That is a very good question."

95

Evie sat down and found herself sinking into the chair. Or rather, sinking into one side of it. She tried to straighten but when that didn't work she decided to prop herself up. Leaning her elbow on the armrest, she cupped her chin and struck up a pensive pose.

"Color. I always seem to remember a book by the color of its binding," Lord Bertram mused.

She couldn't help noticing the books were mostly brown.

"How do you organize your books, Lady Woodridge?" Mr. Carter asked.

"By subject matter. Then again, I don't do it myself. There's a librarian who keeps everything in order. He visits about once a month to sort out the mess I create." As she spoke, Evie sensed Mr. Carter subjecting her to a thorough scrutiny.

She made a point of glancing around the library. On her second sweep of her eyes, she looked at Mr. Carter and asked, "Do you visit Lord Bertram often?"

He gave her a wry smile. "No, not as much as I would like."

"I suppose this is an out of the way place. Do you have far to travel?"

"No, not really."

She persevered with a more pointed remark. "It must be nice to escape the stuffiness of London."

"Yes, I suppose so. I always look forward to some clean country air."

Had he just confirmed he lived in London or had he managed to avoid providing a straight answer?

Lord Bertram yelped. "I've been looking for this tome and it was right under my nose all along." He studied the spine and shook his head. "It's the hazard of living alone. I find myself constantly distracted by things that need attention. I suppose I should ring for tea. Did I already do it?" He walked toward the fireplace and stopped to look at another book. A moment later, he resumed his distracted journey until he finally gave the bell cord a couple of firm tugs. "That ought to get someone's attention. If not, I might need to start bellowing. Sometimes, I fear I have to stir things up to get noticed."

Smiling at his eccentricity, Evie drew her attention away from Lord Bertram and found Mr. Carter still looking at her. Instead of looking away, she held his gaze.

He gave her a brisk smile. "You must forgive me for staring. I've been trying to place you. I'm sure I've seen you somewhere before."

"Perhaps in town," Evie said. "I have a house in Mayfair."

"Yes, perhaps. Although, I'm sure I've seen you recently. Have you been in these parts long?"

"No, I haven't." As he continued to study her, she remembered his look of cruel triumph when he'd won the bid. She didn't think she had read too much into it. There had definitely been a cruel twist to his mouth. Looking at him now, she didn't see any traces of it. In fact, he looked quite friendly.

"Where is that girl?" Lord Bertram thundered.

A second later, the door opened and Alice walked in carrying a tray. She gave Evie a quick glance but did not acknowledge her.

Setting the tray down, she hurried out.

Evie discreetly dislodged herself from the chair and helped herself to a cup of tea. "I don't know what could be taking my friend so long. My dog can't have gone very far. He is quite small."

"I hope you haven't been mistreating your dog," Lord Bertram warned. "That wouldn't do at all."

"Oh, heavens. No. He's a dear, sweet little thing."

"Perhaps we should go outside and help your friend look for it," Mr. Carter suggested but showed no signs of wishing to abandon his cup of tea.

"That might actually be a hindrance. Holmes, that's my dog's name, is rather skittish and quite shy around strangers."

Mr. Carter took a leisurely sip of his tea. "Where did you say you were staying, my lady?"

She hadn't mentioned it. Forced to say something, she decided to stick to the truth. "Nearby, in a hunting lodge."

Lord Bertram snorted. "But it's not hunting season."

"No, we're enjoying some horse riding."

Mr. Carter had the unnerving habit of holding a person's gaze. Without looking away, he spoke to Lord Bertram, "Would you like me to get the door, Bertram?"

His lordship looked confused.

"The door. There is someone at the door," Mr.

Carter clarified.

"Oh, yes. Would you?"

Relieved to be free of Mr. Carter's intense scrutiny, Evie looked at Lord Bertram and found him staring into space and murmuring something she couldn't quite hear.

Footsteps approached and Mr. Carter announced, "The puppy has been found. Bertram, this is Mr. Winchester."

Lord Bertram pulled his attention away from the empty space he'd been studying and looked up at Tom. "How d'you do." After which, he resumed staring into space.

In the time Evie had been observing him, his actions had confirmed Alice's description of him. Evie wouldn't be surprised if he had hidden some of the paintings and objects and forgotten all about them.

She would have to give serious thought to what she would do about his state of isolation. If they could contact his heir, they could enlighten him and suggest something needed to be done. The intrusion might not be entirely welcomed but doing nothing would leave her feeling too unsettled and negligent.

Unless Tom had some pertinent questions to ask, she really didn't see the point of remaining.

Setting her teacup down, she began the process of extricating herself from the chair. Employing as much discretion as possible, she slid her left hand along the armrest. Wrapping her fingers around it, she willed her body to shift to the left.

Seeing her difficulties, Tom sidled up to her and offered her a hand, saying, "The Countess recently came off her horse."

Taking her hand, he gave it a light tug followed by a firmer tug.

"It was a really bad fall," he offered and shifted his hand to grasp Evie by the arm.

Using her free hand to push herself off the chair, she managed to assist in the effort and finally stood on her feet.

Turning, she smiled. "Lord Bertram, thank you for your kind hospitality and forbearance. I hope Mr. Winchester didn't trample on your flower beds."

It appeared to take a moment for his lordship to understand what was happening. "Oh, yes. Yes... You must come again soon. I'm always home. I'll show you out."

Mr. Carter surprised Evie by saying, "Bertram means it. Do come again."

Lord Bertram accompanied them. When they reached the door, Evie again thanked Lord Bertram for his hospitality. She held his gaze for a moment and wondered if, now that they were alone, he might want to say something to her, although what that might be she had no idea.

Lord Bertram fumbled with something in his pocket and finally produced a handkerchief. Looking at it, he seemed to forget why he'd drawn it out. "Yes, well... Have a safe journey and try not to lose your dog again."

CHAPTER 10

When they reached the roadster, Evie turned and saw Lord Bertram still standing at the entrance to Lynchfield Manor. She smiled and waved as she asked Tom, "What took you so long?"

"I lost Holmes."

"Yes, of course, you did."

"I mean, I really lost him. He jumped out of my arms. I chased him around the side of the house and, suddenly, he disappeared." Tom scratched Holmes behind the ears. "He's earned his keep. You'll never guess what he did next."

Still distracted by Lord Bertram, she asked, "He led you to a treasure?" When Tom didn't answer, she looked at him and found him gaping.

"Yes." He held the passenger door open for her and handed Holmes over.

Evie took the puppy and tucked him under her

chin. "What sort of treasure did you find? Oh, wait, don't tell me you found the paintings and missing bits and pieces." She wouldn't be surprised since Lord Bertram struck her as being somewhat absentminded.

"Right again."

"How did you ever manage that?"

"I told you, Holmes led me straight to them." Tom settled behind the wheel and with the engine running, he told her about the motor car being garaged next to the stables where he found the paintings and silver. "Lord Bertram also has a suitcase in his motor car. I think he is ready to make a quick getaway."

"Why would he do that?"

"Your guess is as good as mine."

As Tom put the motor car into gear and drove out at a sedate pace, Evie tried to find a way of explaining Lord Bertram's behavior. "If you ask me, he's probably forgotten he put a suitcase in his car. He doesn't appear to be in good shape. His focus is all over the place." In the same breath, she added, "Then again, he could be pretending to be absentminded." According to Alice Brown, she thought, he had been an entirely different person before the war. The war had left scars on people. How had Lord Bertram been personally affected? Had he lost someone close to him? Or had he simply succumbed to the overall sense of despair over such a tragic time?

"Pretending?" Tom mused.

Yes, indeed. Why would Lord Bertram pretend to be absentminded? How could it possibly benefit him?

When no response came to mind, she changed the subject. "So, what did you make of Mr. Carter's presence?"

"Ah, yes... Mr. Carter. What a strange coincidence. How exactly did he come to be there? Did he say?"

"Lord Bertram knew his father. By the way, I tried to get him to tell me where he lives and he did his best to avoid giving me a straight answer."

"Does that mean you are now suspicious of him?"

"Even if he had told me where he lives I'm sure I would still be suspicious of him. I find it strange that we should see him at the auction and then at Lord Bertram's house."

"Perhaps not so strange since, as you said, he is acquainted with Lord Bertram. For all we know, he just happened to be in the area on his way to visit Lord Bertram and he heard about the auction. We were certainly drawn there for no other reason than curiosity. He might even have heard about the racehorse coming up for sale and decided the opportunity would be too good to miss."

"Are you still pining for the racehorse?"

Tom's jaw clenched and he spoke through gritted teeth. "I wouldn't exactly say I'd been pining for it. But I might be lamenting the missed opportunity."

Evie thought about it for a moment. "For some reason, my instinct tells me there is definitely something odd about Mr. Carter's presence. However..." She hummed under her breath and sent her thoughts in search of clarity.

She sensed Tom glancing at her but he didn't push her for an explanation. As he turned his focus to the road, Evie tried to decipher her thoughts and make sense of her observations.

When Tom slowed down to make a turn she shook her head. "I've had a change of mind. Something Mr. Carter said might compel me to give him the benefit of the doubt."

"Is that my cue to ask what he said?"

"Lord Bertram extended an open invitation to return and Mr. Carter assured me that he meant it. If he is up to no good, surely he would want strangers to stay away so he can carry on with his nefarious activities."

Tom laughed. "I see. He is now on the brink of becoming a villain, at least, in your eyes."

"That's something else. I remember the way he looked when he won the bid for the racehorse. I suspect he has an evil streak. Oh, heavens. I think I've changed my mind again."

"I must have been lost in my despair at having missed out on buying the racehorse for next to nothing. How did Mr. Carter look?"

"Far too pleased with himself in a distorted sort of way." After a moment, she added, "I saw a look of cruel triumph. Yes, that's precisely what I thought at the time."

Tom nodded. "I believe I might have looked the same way if I had been allowed to bid on the horse."

"I somehow doubt it. Yes, yes... it's all coming back

to me. At the time, I remember thinking he looked evil. Almost as if he'd enjoyed taking something valuable from right under the owners' noses." Evie shrugged. "Perhaps I've read too much into it."

They came up to the village and Tom slowed down. "How about a spot of lunch here?"

Evie looked at her watch. "The others will have arrived by now."

"I suppose that is another reason to delay our return. Are we quite ready for them?"

Avoiding a straight answer, she chirped, "Lunch here sounds good."

Even before stepping inside the pub, they could already sense a significant difference from the last time they had been there, only the day before.

A man in a tweed suit stepped out. Seeing them, he gave them an acknowledging nod before going about his business. As the door eased shut, they heard the rise and fall of conservations coming from inside the pub. Glancing through the window, they saw the pub was filled to capacity. Life had returned to the village.

They made their way inside and found a table near a corner. As soon as they sat down, a waiter appeared and, to Evie's surprise, he provided them with a drinking bowl for Holmes.

"This is an easy choice for me," Tom said as he studied the board displaying the menu. "I'll have a game pie, please."

"That sounds enticing. Game pie for me too, please."

The waiter looked down at Holmes.

"I suppose I'll have to start thinking about him too." Looking up at the waiter, she smiled. "Do you think you could find something for him, please?"

When the waiter left, Tom laughed. "I see we are not willing to share from our plates."

"No, we don't want to instill bad habits."

Tom frowned and leaned back, his head tilted slightly.

Evie watched him for a moment and then realized he was eavesdropping on a conversation taking place behind him.

With her impatience growing, she mouthed, "What?"

Still frowning, he leaned forward and whispered, "Mr. Carter took possession of *you know what* straight-away. They were questioning the sale as Mr. Guildford had often been heard saying he had great hopes for the racehorse. In fact, he'd already made plans for the upcoming racing events."

Why had he changed his mind? What Evie still found even more puzzling was that he'd included the horse in the auction instead of selling it through Tattersalls. "Perhaps they are experiencing some unforeseen difficulties."

Their meals were served and a small dish set down on the floor for Holmes.

"I hope you're feeling hungry," Evie said as she settled Holmes beside the dish.

Removing her gloves, she turned her attention to the meal. "I suppose the auction is the talk of the village." And, she thought, everyone would have their own opinion on the matter, but only two people could provide the absolute truth. Mr. and Mrs. Guildford.

Tom studied her for a moment. "You've just had an idea."

"Not really. I was just thinking we might want to contrive a meeting with Mr. and Mrs. Guildford."

"Are we going to lose Holmes again?" Tom asked.

"It worked once, it's bound to work again. I only hope news about our visit to Lord Bertram hasn't spread. Just in case it has, we should put our heads together and see if we can come up with another idea."

"Does this mean we suspect Mr. Carter of some sort of wrongdoing?"

Giving it some thought, Evie said, "I should hate to think this has been a wasted trip. There must be some grounds for Alice Brown's concerns. Which reminds me, we should find a way to speak with her again." Looking at her watch, she cringed. "I'm feeling guilty. The others will have arrived by now. I expect they'll all have something to say about my behavior. I'm afraid I might have created more work for myself. Now I'll have to think how to handle the situation, which is entirely of my own making."

Tom laughed. "From where I'm sitting, it looks like you're drowning in a teacup. You did the best you could. That should be enough. And shame on them if they do criticize you. You're only trying to restore some sort of order."

"You don't seem to understand my concerns. I've

never been distant with people. It simply doesn't suit my character."

"You don't need to tell me about it. You made my job as your chauffeur rather difficult when you insisted on calling me Tom."

Evie gave a determined nod. "I should stick to my guns. If anyone complains, I will simply ignore them. Yes, that's what I'll do."

"Blithely?"

"Yes, indeed."

After a couple of mouthfuls of pie, Tom asked, "Are you likely to ever have a shooting house party again?"

"Oh, heavens. I hadn't given it any thought. Nicholas used to mostly invite people for their skills. I suppose I could go through the old guest lists. Then again, I might just let you do what you like. Mr. Miller would be an excellent source of information. And, since you brought it up, I think it would be a wonderful idea. I know Mr. Miller must miss it dreadfully." Seeing Tom looking rather overwhelmed by her response, Evie added, "Of course, you were probably just making conversation. We don't have to do anything."

"As you said, Mr. Miller must miss it all."

They both looked down at their empty plates.

Evie knew they couldn't linger. The others would be pacing by now and there was also the matter of Detective Evans to deal with. She had no idea how she would tackle that one. However, she supposed it would be practical to find out if Caro knew something about his real identity. For some reason, Evie didn't think she did.

Tom stood up. "I should go take care of the bill."

Evie sat back and sent her gaze skating around the pub. The hum of conversation only stopped briefly when someone walked in. Otherwise, everyone seemed eager to chat. And they did so with great enthusiasm, which made her wonder what they all had to talk about.

"Ready?" Tom asked.

Evie stood up and put her gloves back on. "As ready as I'll ever be."

They walked toward the door. When they reached it, they both stopped, looked at each other and turned.

"And that's something else we'll have to get used to."

Holmes had finished his lunch and had fallen asleep by the empty dish.

And... they had nearly left him behind.

CHAPTER 11

The hunting lodge

*E*vie and Tom sat back and looked at the hunting lodge with its neat little garden and wilderness beyond.

"Ready to face the music?" Tom asked.

"As ready as I'll ever be." Evie saw Mr. Miller approaching from around the corner of the building. He stabbed the ground with his stick and continued walking toward them.

"I have a bad feeling about this," Tom murmured. "Do you?"

"I am, admittedly, on edge. But not as much as Holmes." She looked down at the puppy she held in her arms. "I hope I haven't given him a case of abandonment. He keeps giving me wary glances." Giving him a reassuring smile, she scratched him under his chin. "I promise I'll never leave you behind again."

Mr. Miller reached them and stood looking at them for a moment before saying, "They have all arrived, my lady. But have now left."

That took Evie by surprise. "Left? Where did they go?"

"I couldn't really say, my lady." Mr. Miller dug inside his pocket. "Also, this just arrived. I'd been about to hand it over to the butler."

Evie took the envelope as she asked, "Has the young delivery boy, Eddie, recovered from yesterday's fall?"

Mr. Miller nodded. "He has a few bruises that will take a couple of days to fade and the scraped knee bears a scar. He'll be fine."

Evie turned her attention to the brief letter. "Heavens." Looking at Tom, her eyebrows hitched up. "Alice Brown sent it. While we were having lunch at the pub, the heir arrived at Lynchfield Manor."

"The heir?"

"Nigel Bowles." She turned to Mr. Miller. "Do you know him?"

"I can't say that I do, my lady."

Alice Brown must have panicked and rushed to send the note. What could have prompted him to come right at this time? "Yet another coincidence." Although, Evie felt somewhat reassured by his sudden appearance. He, of all people, would surely look after his lordship's interests. If he saw something wrong with Lord Bertram, he'd surely do something about it. "Well, I suppose we should go in and find out what the others are up to. I'm sure Edgar knows."

Edgar didn't know.

As she pulled a glove off, she asked, "What do you mean?"

"Well, my lady. Shortly after finishing luncheon, they went in to the sitting room and asked for tea. When I returned with the tea, they were no longer there."

Edgar expressed more than a hint of disapproval. Evie guessed he would not have been pleased with being left holding the tea tray.

"No longer there," Evie echoed.

"One of the footmen thought he heard Lady Henrietta say they might as well set out on their own and find their own entertainment."

Heavens. Evie suspected Henrietta's remark had been prompted by their absence.

Belatedly, she wished they had been here to welcome them.

Edgar cleared his throat. He hesitated for a moment and then, said, "The footman also thought he overheard Lady Henrietta say she would like to visit her old friend, Lord Bertram. However, Lady Sara seemed to object and say she would prefer to drive to the village."

The footman seemed to hear quite a lot. And thank goodness. If Henrietta knew Lord Bertram, then that could be an excuse to visit his lordship again. Evie turned to look at Tom. "Of course, Henrietta must know him from his days hunting here."

Tom looked down at the small table beside a wing-back chair where the visitors book he had looked at earlier sat. "I'm sure I closed it."

Someone had been looking through it. Perhaps Henrietta. Evie imagined Henrietta seeing the familiar name and then deciding to use the time here to renew old acquaintances. Although, it seemed strange to set out so soon after arriving. Evie would have thought Henrietta and the others would have been quite eager to find out what she and Tom had been doing.

A moment later, Evie imagined Henrietta feeling incensed because she and Tom hadn't been there to greet them.

When Evie noticed Edgar eyeing Holmes, she introduced him. "He's my new puppy. You'll need to let Mrs. Horace know there'll be an extra mouth to feed." Evie set Holmes down on the floor and gave her other glove a tug. "Edgar, could we please have some tea?"

"Certainly, my lady." Edgar nodded and withdrew from the drawing room.

Evie walked up to the fireplace. When she turned, she found Holmes had followed her. "I don't blame Henrietta for leaving so soon after arriving. I imagine she wants to make sure Toodles enjoys herself."

"That's assuming they managed to free Toodles from her room."

Evie groaned. "I'd forgotten about that. However, Edgar would have mentioned something." She eased down onto the armrest only to surge to her feet again. "No, this won't do. I'm afraid I won't be able to sit and drink tea while the others are out and about doing who knows what."

Despite not finding any clear evidence of wrongdoing, the fact remained they had been called to Lynchfield Manor because Alice Brown thought there might be something amiss. They should not have walked away without delving further.

"What do you suggest we do?" Tom asked, his tone full of intrigue.

Evie snatched the gloves off the table, scooped Holmes into her arms and walked to the door. "Return to Lynchfield Manor, of course."

Taking her coat, Tom helped her into it and they rushed out of the lodge with Evie muttering, "I wish I'd never written those letters."

A moment later, Edgar walked into the sitting room, his attention on the tea tray he carried.

Stopping, he smiled and looked up only to find the room empty. Again.

∿

On the road to Lynchfield Manor

When Evie and Tom reached the village, Evie groaned. "I feel we forgot something." She looked down at Holmes. "Not you, obviously." And thank goodness, she thought.

"How exactly are we going to justify our visit to Lynchfield Manor?" Tom asked.

"I could say I've lost an earring."

"Perhaps I could say I lost a cufflink when I was looking for Holmes."

"That would be very kind of you."

Driving past the village, they followed the narrow road to the manor house.

Tom slowed down and gave the right of way to a horse and cart coming from the opposite direction. Looking over his shoulder, he said, "There's another motor car coming. I hope they slow down."

With the road clear, they continued on. Just before he turned to drive through the pillared entrance, Tom looked over his shoulder again.

"What is it?" Evie asked.

"That driver must have sped up straight after overtaking the horse and cart." Shrugging, he continued on, driving along the narrow drive. When the house appeared, they saw Edmonds leaning against the Duesenberg, reading a newspaper. He looked up and straightened.

"Why doesn't Edmonds look surprised to see us?"

Tom laughed. "His lack of surprise at seeing you might have to do with your shenanigans. Or he might be trying to remember everything he needs to tell you."

"Shenanigans? I take exception to that."

"You can't deny being secretive and underhanded."

"No, I suppose you're right."

Tom climbed out of the roadster and opened the

door for Evie. "So, how are we going to do this? Do I have to disappear around the side of the house and pretend I'm looking for my cufflink while you go inside and explain?"

"That sounds like a solid plan. But first I'd like to hear what Edmonds has to say."

They walked up to him. Evie introduced him to Holmes and just as she was about to ask if he had any news, they all heard a motor car drive up.

"That's the motor I saw driving behind us," Tom said. "It was either following us or they just happen to be headed to the same destination."

"The same destination? That's rather odd." Evie looked at Tom, her eyebrow slightly raised.

They both said, "Coincidence?"

Hardly, Evie thought.

When the driver opened the door to climb out, Evie shielded her eyes against the sun.

However, Tom identified the driver first. "This is interesting."

"Good heavens," Evie exclaimed and pursed her lips.

The driver approached them. "Lady Woodridge. Mr. Winchester."

"Detective," Tom said while Evie remained silent.

Detective Evans had a lot of explaining to do, she thought. The contents of the letter she had received a couple of days before bounced around her mind, reminding her how cross she was with him.

"I got lost along the way then I saw you drive by," the detective explained. "At least, I thought it was you.

So I decided to follow." Detective Evans looked up at the house. "Nice place you have."

"This isn't the hunting lodge," Evie said, her tone hard.

"Oh?"

Tom interjected, "The house belongs to Viscount Bertram."

"My apologies. I assumed you were headed to the hunting lodge. I came up as soon as I received your telegram, my lady. I had actually been staying not far from here. When the message finally made its way to me, I thought it sounded rather urgent."

He'd been staying nearby? Caro hadn't mentioned it. "I assume Caro didn't know. Do you make a habit of keeping her in the dark?" About his whereabouts and the rest, Evie thought.

Detective Evans looked puzzled.

Knowing she had been rather abrupt, Evie experienced a moment of remorse. However, she brushed the feeling away. Detective Evans hadn't been entirely honest with them. She had good reason to be annoyed with him. While she had been preparing to tackle him head on, she had expected to deal with Henrietta first as she suspected the Dowager would have a great deal to complain about. But now would be as good a time as any to give the detective a piece of her mind. A huge chunk of it.

The detective looked uneasy. "I'm afraid you have the advantage, my lady."

Evie lifted her chin. "It has come to our attention—"

Evie stopped and tried to rephrase the accusation. "What I mean to say is that you haven't been entirely..." Again, she broke off. She couldn't very well accuse the detective of being dishonest. There were many things she didn't mention about her private life and that didn't make her dishonest. She tried again. "There are some things we assumed about you and now we realize we were quite misinformed. And the fact the information hasn't become common knowledge worries us."

"Information? About what exactly, my lady?"

"You, of course."

The detective frowned. "Indeed. Alas, I'm afraid I'm still not sure what you mean."

Tom stepped in. "What the Countess means to say—"

The sound of a hard thump had them all turning. Before anyone could say anything, they heard a sharp shriek.

They all turned toward the house.

"Did you hear that?" Evie asked.

"How could I not hear it? Did it come from inside the house?" Tom asked.

"I'm not sure it did." Evie looked toward the side of the house.

The detective stepped forward and headed straight for the front door which, to their surprise, stood open.

Evie and Tom followed. Without looking over her shoulder, Evie knew Edmonds had also followed, the sound of his footsteps on the gravel declaring his determination to see what the commotion had been about for himself.

They heard the shriek again, followed by a loud exclamation. This prompted them to rush across the hall. As they did so, Henrietta, Sara and Toodles appeared at the library door.

By the time Henrietta found her voice and demanded, "What on earth is going on?" Evie and Tom had disappeared as they continued toward the sound of the frightful shrieks. Unfortunately, Edmonds hadn't moved quickly enough. As they disappeared down the hall, Evie heard Henrietta asking him to explain what had happened.

They made it all the way to the rooms at the back of the house and the kitchen where they found the door open. The detective was a few steps ahead of them and they hurried to catch up. Running out the back door, they almost scattered in different directions when the shriek pierced the air again.

The odd intervals between shrieks surprised Evie until they rounded the side of the house and saw Alice Brown standing with one hand clutching the side of her skirt and flapping it about while the other hand pointed ahead of her.

She seemed to be having some sort of reaction to something.

Several more steps brought them up to her and the sight in front of her.

Evie stumbled back. "Good heavens."

"It's Viscount Bertram," Tom said.

CHAPTER 12

*E*vie tore her attention away from the sight of Lord Bertram's lifeless body and looked at Alice Brown. The young woman's shoulders appeared to be quite tense while her right hand remained pointing toward the body.

Stepping forward, Evie put her hands around her shoulders. "Alice."

Alice Brown didn't move or respond. Thinking she hadn't heard her, Evie persevered. "Alice, you should come inside now."

Detective Evans and Tom had crouched down and now blocked the view yet Alice seemed reluctant or unable to move.

Evie glanced up at the house. There were two windows directly above but both appeared to be closed. She pushed her gaze up and looked at the roof.

Shaking her head, she turned her attention back to

Alice Brown again. Encouraging her, Evie managed to guide her back inside. The young woman's feet dragged along the ground. She appeared to be in a trance with her eyes wide and her lips slightly parted. Denial and shock, Evie thought.

As they reached the back door, a housemaid came rushing out and demanded, "What's happened? I heard a scream."

Evie managed to say, "I think we'll need some strong tea, please."

The young housemaid hesitated. Then, clutching her apron she swung around and ran back inside.

Evie followed, her hands still around Alice's shoulders. She understood the young woman's shock. She'd only had a brief look at the body and yet it had made quite an impact, the finality of death dulling her senses.

As they entered the house Evie heard the crunch of footsteps approaching. Glancing over her shoulder, she saw Detective Evans hurrying toward them.

"I will need to telephone the local constabulary," he said. "Do you know if there is a telephone here?"

"There's bound to be one."

Inside, they headed to the kitchen. Evie drew out a chair and encouraged Alice to sit down. Turning to the other maid, she asked about the telephone.

"There's one in the library."

Evie heard the detective make his way toward the library. Meanwhile, the housemaid poured the tea and set the cup in front of Alice.

"That was quick," Evie remarked.

"The kettle was half full and the water still quite hot." She looked at Alice. "What's wrong with her? She's not blinking."

"I think she might be in shock," Evie offered.

"I heard the screams," the maid said. "But I couldn't tell where they came from so I rushed around the house. I'd been dusting." She signaled over her shoulder. "There's another pot of tea already made so I assume Alice did that."

That, Evie thought, meant she must have been in the kitchen.

Just then, Alice's arm shot out again and she pointed toward the window which faced the side of the house.

Heavens. Had she seen the body fall?

Evie dismissed the thought and focused on Alice. With the help of the maid, they managed to get her to take a sip of tea.

Footsteps thumped along the hallway. A moment later, a man Evie didn't recognize came bounding through the kitchen and, without sparing them a glance, he went out the back door.

"That's Mr. Nigel Bowles," the maid whispered.

Evie heard him skid to a stop and, judging by the sound of his hollow moan, she thought he might eventually need something stronger than tea.

She then saw Tom walk past the window, his hand clasped around Mr. Nigel Bowles' shoulder and assumed Tom had thought it best if the heir returned to the house.

They walked in and headed toward the front of the house.

"I think I should go and see if they need anything," the maid suggested.

As Alice took another sip of tea, Evie said, "That must have been quite a shock, Alice. Are you feeling better?"

She produced a small nod but didn't say anything. After finishing the tea, she sat back and looked toward the window.

To Evie's surprise, she spoke.

"I was standing by the window, waiting for the tea to steep when I saw something fall down. At first, I thought it was a bird swooping down. A moment later... maybe a second or two, I realized I've never seen such a large bird."

Alice fell silent again. She continued looking at the window and Evie imagined she still held the image of what she'd seen in her mind.

Calling on all her patience, Evie gave her time to compose herself.

Alice blinked and appeared to snap out of the trance. She took a hard swallow and followed it with a deep intake of breath. She turned to look at Evie, her eyes wide and her voice sounding hollow as she said, "He fell. His lordship fell."

Evie couldn't bring herself to confirm the obvious.

She didn't think Alice needed it to be confirmed. Rather, she thought Alice might be trying to come to terms with what she'd seen.

The other housemaid returned to the kitchen and stood by in silence, her hands clasped against her chest.

Feeling helpless, Evie searched for something appropriate to say and could only come up with, "Would you like another cup of tea?"

Alice shook her head. "I'd been daydreaming. Just looking at the garden and thinking I should cut some flowers. He didn't make a sound."

Shuddering, the housemaid swung around and walked to the stove. "I'll put the kettle on."

Just as she thought Alice would say more, Evie heard someone approaching. Looking up, she saw Detective Evans standing at the door.

She stood up and went to stand beside him. "Did you manage to contact the police?"

He nodded. "They should be along soon. But we'll have to wait a while for the detectives to arrive."

Of course, the small village would be lucky to have a couple of constables, if that.

"Has she said anything?" he asked.

Evie told him the little Alice had revealed. The fact Lord Bertram had fallen to his death in silence struck her as odd. "Why do you think he didn't make a sound?"

"It's possible he jumped or…"

"Or what?" Evie encouraged.

"He might already have been dead when he fell."

"He had guests." Even to her own ears it sounded like an unreasonable remark. Almost as if she thought people shouldn't kill themselves or allow themselves to be killed if they had company. "Have you spoken to the others?"

"No, not yet." He signaled toward Alice. "Do you think she's up to talking?"

"She might still be in shock but she spoke without any encouragement so she might be ready to say more or you might be able to coax some information out of her."

Looking at the other housemaid, he asked, "Would you give us a moment, please?"

Wiping her hands, the housemaid hurried out of the kitchen. While Evie made her way to the library where she hoped to find the others. She remembered Tom had come this way with Nigel Bowles so she expected to find him in the library.

When she reached the door, she stopped and turned to look across the hall at the front door.

When they'd arrived, it had stood open. She entertained a couple of possibilities.

Since Lord Bertram didn't have a footman at the moment, he might have opened the door, invited his guests inside and simply walked on ahead without bothering to close the door and either Toodles, Sara or Henrietta, not accustomed to closing doors because there was always a footman to do so, had merely ignored it. Or someone else might have walked in or out after their arrival. She would only know for sure once she talked to the others.

As she turned to enter the library, she saw a shape move past one of the windows facing the front of the house. Stopping again, she looked toward the front door.

Mr. Roland Carter walked in and left the door open. Looking up, he saw Evie and stopped dead on his tracks.

"Lady Woodridge?" For a moment, he looked surprised to see her there. He glanced over his shoulder and then back at Evie. "Yes, of course. Mr. Winchester... I just saw him outside. Dreadful business."

So, Tom had gone outside again. "Was he alone?"

"No, Nigel Bowles is with him. Although, I have no idea why. The man is distraught. I told him to come inside, but he wouldn't hear of it."

Mr. Carter walked toward her, shaking his head as if in disbelief. "What do you make of this nasty business?"

"Quite dreadful. I can't even begin to imagine how it happened. We'd only just arrived when we heard the scream." She studied him for a moment. Despite expressing his concerns and disbelief, he appeared to be well composed. "Where were you when it happened?"

He looked away as if distracted and then said, "Upstairs. In my room. I needed to attend to some correspondence and then I fell asleep on my chair. The scream woke me up but I thought I'd imagined it. Then I heard it again."

Evie frowned. "Is that when you came downstairs?" They had been outside and it had taken them a moment to react and rush inside the house. Evie didn't remember seeing him.

"No, I'm afraid I scrambled to my feet and hesitated. I couldn't make out where the scream had come from. At first, I went to look out of the window facing the front garden and then I went to the door and eased it open. I'm embarrassed to say I was still a little dazed. I remember hearing footsteps along the hallway. A moment later, I came down and went to the library. That's when Lady Woodridge... That is, the other Lady Woodridge confirmed there had indeed been a scream. Several of them, in fact." He turned and signaled toward the front door. "I went out that way. I'm afraid I headed in the wrong direction. Eventually, I made my way around the other side of the house and found Mr. Winchester and Nigel Bowles standing over his lordship. Of course, at the time, I didn't know it was Bertram. I must admit I went into an immediate state of denial. How could it have happened?"

How indeed.

Everything Mr. Carter had told her suggested he had come downstairs after they had arrived. Well after if he had found Tom and Nigel Bowles outside. By then, she had already encouraged Alice inside the house.

"The police will be arriving shortly," she assured him. "I'm sure they'll get to the bottom of it."

"Oh, yes. Yes, of course." Clearing his throat, he said, "I hear there is a detective present."

"Yes, he's known to us. He came up to meet us and... Well, it's a long story."

"I see." He fumbled with something in his pocket. Looking over her shoulder, he then said, "If you'll excuse me. I need to go look for something strong to drink."

Evie suggested he avoid the kitchen. "The detective is interviewing the housemaid." She had no idea where Mr. Carter would find a fortifying drink but since he'd been staying at the house she assumed he would know.

Turning, she heaved in a deep breath and walked into the library. Time to face the others, she thought.

"There she is." Henrietta stood up. "We didn't dare go out there. I'm sure it's a ghastly sight, enough to give anyone nightmares."

Toodles sat on the chair Evie had sunk into earlier in the day. She looked somewhat lopsided and aggrieved.

"Don't mind Toodles," Henrietta said. "She's been struggling with that chair for some time now."

"I take it you know what's happened," Evie managed to push the words out.

"Yes, of course. Detective Evans told us when he came in to use the telephone."

Evie took a moment to put all the pieces together and remembered she'd been in the kitchen with Alice

Brown when the detective had come in and asked to use the telephone.

"Do we know how it happened?" Henrietta asked.

Sara hushed Henrietta. "Can't you see Evie is in shock. She probably has the image stamped in her mind."

"Oh, my goodness," Henrietta exclaimed. "Did you see him?"

"Yes, I'm afraid so. I rushed outside with the others."

Henrietta shuddered. "You should sit down but be careful. These chairs are treacherous."

Evie chose to stand by the fireplace. "Did the detective ask you any questions when he came in to use the telephone?"

Henrietta looked affronted. "No, why would he? We've been here all along. Surely you don't think we had anything to do with Bertram's death."

"Of course, you didn't. But... Well... I'm just thinking..." Evie rubbed her temple. Something quite obvious sprung out at her. They were all witnesses. "What can you tell me? Why wasn't Lord Bertram here with you?"

"We'd been talking," Sara explained. "Suddenly, he got up and left to fetch something. It's hard to say what because he mumbled a great deal and he jumped from subject to subject. In any case, I'd given up listening to him."

"I'd been asking Julius about his predecessor," Henrietta admitted.

"Who is Julius?" Evie asked.

"Lord Bertram, of course. He's the one we're talking about. Anyhow, I couldn't remember the last time I'd seen Alexander and Bertram said something about a photograph or was it a journal? I can't remember which and I think he went out to get one or the other."

"Did you see in which direction he turned?" Evie asked.

"What do you mean?"

Evie explained about arriving with Tom and stopping to talk with the detective and finding the front door open. While she didn't mention it, she also remembered during her earlier visit Lord Bertram had headed in one direction only to change his mind.

"Now that you mention it, why is the detective with you?" Henrietta asked.

"Oh, heavens. It's a long story." Forgetting about the treacherous chairs, Evie lowered herself into a chair and unfortunately found herself sinking into it.

"I warned you. Not to worry, we'll heave-ho you out of it."

"So, do you remember in which direction he headed?" Evie asked again.

"No, I'm afraid I was preoccupied with finding a comfortable spot on my chair. It's rather lumpy."

Evie looked down at Holmes and lost herself for a moment, taking comfort in holding the little puppy. Distracted, she asked, "Did Tom and Nigel Bowles come in here?"

"No."

"That's strange. I thought they came in here to look

for a drink." Evie looked around the library and saw a table in a corner with several bottles. She supposed they'd headed straight out again. Nigel Bowles must have been in the throes of denial and determined to see Lord Bertram again.

Sara gasped. "Oh, is that a dog?"

Evie looked down. She held Holmes against her chest and for a moment worried she might have come close to choking him. "Yes, he's a gift from Tom. His name is Holmes."

"I take it you have high aspirations for him," Henrietta remarked.

"As a matter of fact, Holmes has already earned his keep." Evie explained about their earlier visit. Belatedly, she remembered she had decided to keep their investigation a secret. Although, that had now become a moot point.

Henrietta and Sara exchanged a knowing look. "She's on a case." Looking at her, they both asked, "Are you?"

Instead of answering, Evie turned to her grandmother. "How are you, Grans?"

Toodles harrumphed. "I'm currently stuck in a chair. Some might say it's an improvement on being locked up in my room and being prevented from leaving the estate."

"Yes, I heard about that. Who would do such a thing?" Evie asked, her voice full of innocence.

"Who indeed."

Sara turned her attention to a dusty tome while

Henrietta fiddled with her necklace. "Yes, we all thought it quite extraordinary. I blame those bright young things gallivanting around the countryside and playing tricks on people. Evangeline, you should instruct your servants to keep a look out for them. You never know who might wander in through the front door..."

CHAPTER 13

The library
Lynchfield Manor

*E*vie didn't want to disrupt the detective's conversation with Alice and she assumed Tom was still busy consoling the heir, Nigel Bowles, so she remained in the library.

Holding Holmes in her arms offered a comforting alternative to sitting in a corner and losing herself in a meditative trance. Her steady, gentle strokes went a long way toward calming her mind.

So far, Evie thought, Toodles had been the only one to mention what had happened after she and Tom had left Halton House. Although, she hadn't explained what had actually triggered the curious events.

Instead of pushing for more information, Evie

decided it would be best to let them sort it all out themselves. However, knowing her granny, she must have taken exception to something said and had decided to take matters into her own hands. After which, the Dowagers had reciprocated by locking her up in her room.

To her relief, no one brought up the subject of the letters she had issued.

Holmes fell asleep in her arms so Evie had nothing else to distract her. They sat in the library for a good fifteen minutes before the police finally arrived, followed by an ambulance. The fact no one spoke suggested they were all preoccupied with what had happened to Lord Bertram.

"At last," Henrietta exclaimed. "I can't bear all this waiting around in silence. It forces one into introspection and I find the strangest thoughts weaving into my mind. I have a sudden craving for lemon cake."

"Perhaps I can distract you," Evie offered. "How well did you know Lord Bertram?"

Henrietta looked about her as if searching for a suitable response. "As well as one knows anyone you only see every so often. I don't recall him being a good shot. Yet, he always made an appearance at the lodge. If I think about it, he was the type of man who hovered in the background echoing everyone's sentiments. By that, I mean that he never really had anything original or clever to say." She glanced at Sara. "I hope my remarks are not taken the wrong way. I don't wish to speak ill of the dead."

Toodles tried to shift in her seat and gave up. "If we have to stay here any longer, perhaps we should help ourselves to a fortifying drink."

"Out of the question," Henrietta declared. "If we start drinking now, we'll never dislodge you from that chair."

Sensing her granny's rising impatience with the situation, Evie turned to Henrietta and tried to change the subject. "Can you remember anything else about the conversation you were having before Lord Bertram stepped out of the room? Actually, did he remember you?"

"Yes, of course. Although, he said something odd. He referred to me as the real Countess of Woodridge."

Sara rolled her eyes. "I should have taken exception to that."

Evie wondered if Lord Bertram had thought of her as a fake Countess of Woodridge. "Did he seem pleased to see you?"

Henrietta gave it some thought. "Yes, I believe so. In fact, we appeared to have arrived at a most opportune moment." She turned to Sara. "Did you notice how the other fellow excused himself? What's his name... Mr. Cart something or other."

"Mr. Roland Carter." Sara nodded. "He seemed to be eager to avoid our company. Then again, we had been arguing in the motor car so we must have looked rather frightful. Toodles scowled all the way from London. There, I said it."

Evie knew this particular subject couldn't be

avoided any longer. "Granny? Is something the matter?"

"Only that I had a grand journey all mapped out in the spur of the moment and these two ruined it for me."

"Oh, where were you going?"

"Venice or the Riviera. Anywhere but here since I seem to have overstayed my welcome." She gave Sara a pointed look. "There, *I've* said it."

So, she had been right and it looked as though Sara had indeed remarked on Toodles' lengthy stay.

Not to be outdone, Henrietta stepped forward. "Since we are airing our grievances, I should like to say I am not at all happy to be issued orders, even if they happen to come from the head of the house."

"You said you were pleased about coming up here because it's been so long since your last visit," Sara declared. "And the letters certainly gave us something to talk about. In fact, I remember you saying they had been a welcome relief from the tedium we'd been experiencing."

Heavens. One simple question had wrenched open a can of... misgivings.

Sara craned her neck and looked toward the window. "Oh, it looks like something is happening. I see a couple of policemen walking past the window."

Henrietta joined her in looking out of the window. "Yes, I believe they are carrying a stretcher to the ambulance."

Evie tried to see but she became stuck in her chair

and in her effort to lift herself up, she ended up sinking lower into it.

To her relief, Tom came to her rescue. He walked in and headed straight to the fireplace where Evie sat.

"Thank heavens." Evie took his hand and, with his help, extricated herself from the chair. "What news do you have?"

"Nigel Bowles is inconsolable. I brought him inside thinking he could do with a drink and he ended up rushing out the front door to look at the body again. He simply refuses to believe what's happened. The local doctor came along with the ambulance and is now tending to him. I heard him mention sedatives."

"Did Nigel Bowles say anything about where he'd been when his lordship fell?"

"He mentioned something about inspecting the house and looking around the attic. He's been doing it during his last couple of visits. He actually said something about Lord Bertram deteriorating and becoming more forgetful."

"Did he have other health issues?"

"Nigel Bowles didn't say exactly and I didn't feel it appropriate to ask."

Evie lowered her voice. "The detective suggested his lordship might have been dead before falling. That would certainly raise more questions."

Henrietta drew their attention by asking, "Will the detective interrogate us?"

"He might wish to ask a few questions." Tom looked around the room.

"If you're looking for the drinks, they are in the corner," Evie said.

"No, I'm fine. I was just thinking…" He held her gaze for a moment. "I wonder if this has anything to do with Alice Brown's concerns."

"That is a good question. The detective has been with her for quite some time. She took the death really hard." Evie fell silent and thought about Mr. Roland Carter and the heir. They had both been upstairs and Lord Bertram has obviously fallen from somewhere upstairs.

Evie nudged Tom and signaled toward the door. Turning to the others, she said, "We'll be back shortly."

"What is it?" Tom asked as they walked out into the hall.

"I wouldn't mind going upstairs to look around. I'm sure the detective won't mind. I'm curious about the windows. When I was outside, I looked up and I'm sure they were both closed."

As they walked up the stairs, Tom said, "By the way, I noticed you struggled to find the words to confront the detective when he first arrived."

Evie grumbled, "I wish you hadn't reminded me. It's obvious I need to work on my confrontational skills. I'm fairly certain *Detective Evans* knew exactly what I'd been referring to."

"Interesting. I didn't get that impression. In fact, I think you succeeded in frightening him."

Evie's eyes sparkled. "Really? Oh, I do hope so."

"I still think you should give him the benefit of the doubt."

They reached the first landing and Tom tested the window. "It's definitely closed. In fact, it's stuck."

They continued on to the next floor. When they reached the window, they peered down and saw the detective standing where the body had landed.

Tom tried to open the window and again found it stuck.

"Well, that's that." Except, it couldn't be. Lord Bertram had fallen from either one of these two windows.

They both turned, looked up and saw the stairs leading to a door.

"Do you think that's the roof?" Evie asked.

"It's either the roof or the attic and there's only one way to find out."

They walked up the remaining steps and stood outside the door for a moment. Finally, Tom reached for the door handle. The door opened and they saw the sky.

"It's the rooftop." Tom pushed out a breath.

Evie frowned. "Why would Lord Bertram come up here? Had he suffered a moment of disorientation? I'm not sure we should go out there," Evie warned. "I know parts of the rooftop at Halton House have gravel on it. If this one does too, we might disrupt footprints."

Tom nodded in agreement.

They started walking down only to stop when they heard someone coming up.

A moment later, the detective appeared. "I thought I saw someone looking down from a window. Did you find anything of interest?"

"Most definitely." Tom pointed over his shoulder. "The windows are stuck and there's a door leading to the rooftop. We thought we should wait for you."

The detective dug inside his coat pocket and produced a notebook. After making some notes, he looked up. "Right. Well, I suppose I should go up and see."

"We'll wait here," Evie said, her tone dutiful.

"Are you afraid of heights, Lady Woodridge?"

"Not at all. I just assume you don't wish to have the area disturbed."

"I'm sure we'll be fine so long as you walk behind me. In fact, I would appreciate more eyes on the scene. You are both quite good observers."

Forgetting her grievances, Evie brightened. "Oh, thank you, detective."

The detective went through first and they followed at a discreet distance walking along the narrow paths hedging the parapet. The smooth surface on the roof failed to reveal anything of significance. With no obvious footprints, they walked to the ledge lined with urns and looked down.

"This should be the spot."

Evie and Tom looked around but didn't see anything to suggest someone had stood at that spot and considered ending their life.

Stepping closer to the ledge, Evie studied the urns.

They all had layers of aging with moss and soot from the chimneys.

"Oh, could this be something?"

"What?" the detective asked.

She pointed to the ground. "There are traces of moss. It might have been scraped off... Yes, here." She then pointed to the urn. "It's almost as if someone scratched their nail on the surface."

She pictured Lord Bertram standing there and resting his hand on the urn, perhaps considering what he'd been about to do.

"He could have been standing here and someone came up behind him," the detective mused. He looked up. "The sun is on the other side so he couldn't have been blinded by it."

If he had been, Evie thought, he might have lost his footing.

She brushed her fingertips along the surface and then inspected them. Soot. "Did you happen to notice any dirt or traces of moss on his lordship's fingers? It could confirm his presence on the roof."

The detective drew out his notebook and made a note of it. "I'll have to look into it."

"We met him earlier today and he appeared to be in a strange state." Evie tried to find the words to explain his behavior. "Almost as if his mind had been elsewhere."

The detective shook his head. "This might be ruled death by misadventure."

Nothing but an unfortunate incident? Evie couldn't quite accept it.

"Then again, it's not really my place to say," the detective added and checked his watch.

"Are you still waiting for the local detective to arrive?"

"Yes, this is not my jurisdiction."

"Death by misadventure... Is your colleague likely to reach that conclusion without delving further?" Tom asked.

"I can't tell him how to perform his duty, but I'm sure he'll want to talk to everyone who's been here today."

Evie didn't expect him to share any of his findings but she thought it might be worth a try. "Did you get anything out of Alice Brown?"

The detective turned away from the ledge and guided them back down. "She told me she'd reached out to Lotte Mannering. Apparently, she read about the lady detective in a newspaper." He glanced at Evie. "Is that why you were here?"

"Yes, indeed. Tom and I followed up on Alice Brown's concerns but we only managed to witness his lordship's odd behavior."

Reaching the ground floor, they returned to the library and found Henrietta and Sara struggling to pull Toodles out of the clutches of the chair.

Henrietta released her hand. "It's no use. I'm afraid she's stuck." Looking up, she saw Evie and smiled.

"We've been quite ambitious but we lack the physical strength."

Tom rushed to assist them and managed to free Toodles who stood up and straightened her coat with a huff.

Giving Henrietta a pointed look, Toodles muttered, "I know you enjoyed that a great deal, Henrietta. You know the tables will turn. If not today, then someday soon."

Henrietta's eyes twinkled. "And then the fat lady will sing?" As soon as the words spilled out, Henrietta looked contrite. "My apologies. After all, we are responsible for feeding you all those cakes."

"That was uncalled for, Henrietta," Sara chided. "Toodles is not fat. That chair simply happens to be devious."

Evie hid her smile. Seeing the detective walking to the telephone, she suggested giving him a moment of silence so he could make his call.

Their silence lasted only a few minutes.

Henrietta sidled up to Evie. "Are you going to keep us in the dark?"

Evie wouldn't dare since that would only prompt them to pursue their own investigation. "I'll tell you everything we know when we return to the hunting lodge. I believe there's nothing more for us to do here."

CHAPTER 14

"*A*re we all present and accounted for?" Tom asked as they settled into the roadster.

"We most certainly are. I doubt Holmes would forgive me if I left him behind again. Drive on, please."

Detective Evans had been surprised by their departure. More so since he had now been put in charge of the investigation until further notice. She supposed he'd expected them to linger and push their way in but Evie felt they needed to step back and let him do his job. Besides, she had her family squabbles to deal with...

In reality, Evie felt she had already failed since she had tried to address Alice Brown's concerns and had found nothing wrong. Certainly nothing to suggest Lord Bertram's life had been in danger.

Evie suspected the detective had been glad of the opportunity to take over the investigation since it delayed his arrival at the hunting lodge. Despite giving the impression he hadn't understood what she'd been alluding to, Evie felt sure he knew she still had a bone to pick with him.

Losing herself in her thoughts, she wondered if she should encourage Caro to visit her family who lived nearby. Of course, it would mean having to rely on Millicent but Evie would happily sacrifice her sanity to keep Caro happy and distracted while she dealt with the detective.

Tom leaned toward her. "You're plotting."

"How can you tell?"

"Your eyebrows are set into a scowl and your lips are puckered up."

"I had no idea I had a plotting expression. In any case, I realize the detective will be preoccupied with the case so I will simply have to bide my time."

"I see your mood hasn't mellowed."

"No. This matter has to be faced head on and the issue addressed before Caro's heart is broken."

Once again, Tom tried to convince her they couldn't and shouldn't jump to conclusions.

Evie looked into Holmes' eyes and took comfort in the feeling of unconditional love. "Poor Alice. I hope Nigel Bowles keeps her on. Otherwise, she'll have to find another place of employment."

"Nigel Bowles?" Tom's eyebrows drew down. "I assumed he had made his way into your list of suspects."

"I don't have one of those and... Why do you think he's a person of interest?" Evie gasped. "Oh, when Lord Bertram fell to his death, he'd been upstairs."

"That's right."

Had his reaction to Lord Bertram's death been an act? "Did you hear him say anything suspicious?"

Tom gave it some thought. "Too soon. Yes, I'm sure I heard him say that when he bent over the body."

Had he been referring to Lord Bertram's age or to something else? Evie remembered Alice saying Lord Bertram hadn't had any children so the heir, Nigel Bowles, was a distant relative. Perhaps he'd only now started to become better acquainted with Lord Bertram.

"Oh, heavens. What if Nigel Bowles had something to do with the death? Alice will definitely lose her position."

Tom glanced at her and smiled. "I'm sure you'll think of something."

They arrived at the hunting lodge just as the others were walking inside. Henrietta stopped and tugged Sara who reached out and grabbed hold of Toodles. They all turned to look at them.

"I think they're talking about us," Evie said.

"Just as we are talking about them?" Tom laughed. "What could they possibly be saying?"

"Holmes and I don't care for your mocking tone, Mr. Winchester. Anyhow, if they are up to something, it will all have to wait because I need to speak with Caro."

They took their time going inside the house. Evie

set Holmes down and watched him as he sniffed around. His interest came and went and in-between, he appeared to doze off. "I suppose we can't delay this any longer." She bent down and scooped him up.

When they reached the front door, they both thought they saw Henrietta peeking out of a window.

"Where are you going?" Tom asked when he saw Evie heading away from the drawing room.

"Upstairs to talk with Caro."

"And you expect me to go in to the drawing room by myself?"

Evie smiled at him. "Like a lamb to the slaughter."

Turning, Evie felt a weight lift off her. So much had happened, she actually looked forward to escaping to her room.

Going up the stairs, Evie's steps faltered. She would need to tread with care and, somehow, find out how much Caro knew about the detective without revealing what she now knew about him.

She looked heavenward. When had her life become so complicated?

As she came up to the door to her room, she leaned in and pressed her ear to the door only to hear Millicent's familiar voice.

"I told you I heard their motor driving up."

Evie pictured her standing by the window and signaling to the roadster.

"She'll be here any minute now and you still haven't cleaned up that mess."

Mess? Good heavens. What on earth had happened this time?

"Another scent bottle broken," Millicent continued. "Her ladyship should take that out of your wages."

"I would not have dropped it if you hadn't startled me. Why must you shadow my every move?"

That was definitely Caro.

"You've been daydreaming again," Millicent accused. "That's why you dropped it. What will her ladyship say if she hears us bickering?"

"Since you're the only one bickering she will say you've made her job easy in deciding which one of us she will keep."

"You're not still going on about that. You know very well she intends getting rid of you."

In truth, Evie hadn't really given much thought to what Caro would do after she married, probably because she didn't expect Caro to continue working, but she seemed determined to do so.

Had Caro given any real thought to it? What if she harbored doubts and she hadn't been able to talk about them?

Evie looked down at Holmes and pushed out a long breath.

What if Caro knew about the detective's real identity and refused to face the reality of its full meaning? Her attitude appeared to suggest it.

This complicated matters. If she tackled the issue, Caro might not want to talk about it. But if she left it alone, Caro might end up making the wrong decision.

Evie eased the door open and stepped inside. Setting Holmes down on the floor, she walked to her dresser. Caught by surprise, Caro rushed to tidy the bedside table while Millicent stepped back until her back bumped against the wall.

Evie greeted them and sat at her dresser. She introduced them to Holmes who made a point of sniffing them before curling up by her feet. "Did you enjoy your train journey up here?"

They both gushed about the sceneries they had enjoyed looking at.

Before they could fall into an awkward silence, Evie decided she needed to establish how far along in the relationship Caro was. "Caro, have you given any thought to your trousseau?"

"Milady, Henry hasn't asked me yet."

"But you know he will. You must have talked at great length about your plans and your future together." She glanced over her shoulder in time to see Caro's cheeks coloring.

"As a matter of fact, we have. There's just the formality of the proposal."

Heavens. They had made plans for the future. Surely the detective wouldn't dangle an enticing carrot and then withdraw it. He couldn't possibly be so cruel.

Was Tom right to suggest she needed to give him the benefit of the doubt?

Yes, most likely.

Evie removed her earrings and considered her next

words. "Millicent, would you run down and fetch a bowl of water for Holmes, please?"

As soon as Millicent hurried out of the room, Evie turned and said, "Caro, I hope you don't feel I'm over-stepping."

"Oh, never, milady."

"Has the detective made a firm commitment to you by talking openly about marriage or has it only been implied?"

"Well, we've talked about where we're going to live. He's actually looking for a cottage near Halton House."

How could he make such firm plans and not reveal the truth about himself? Caro would definitely not be able to work as her maid. Didn't she realize that?

The drawing room

Evie edged the door to the drawing room open and walked in just as Sara said, "You should have listened to me. If you had, we would not have been witnesses to that horrible death. Now the detective will want to speak with us and who knows what truths he'll wrench out of us."

"Heavens, Sara." Henrietta clucked her tongue. "You make it sound as if he will twist your words into a confession. In any case, the alternative, if you recall, didn't sit well with you."

Sara huffed, "I thought you held Lady Hansen in high esteem."

"Yes, but it's not about me. You're the one who doesn't care to spend an afternoon in her medieval manor."

Evie remembered Louisa Hansen who lived nearby. A lovely woman with a soft voice and a passion for everything medieval. Visiting her meant stepping back in time and drinking tea from pewter mugs and listening to her playing the lyre. Evidently, they had considered visiting her instead of Lord Bertram.

"Ah, here she is," Henrietta exclaimed.

"Has someone rang for tea?" Evie asked, her tone nonchalant.

"We certainly have but Edgar didn't believe we wanted tea. I don't know what's come over your butler. I thought you had sorted everyone out with your letters. Perhaps you were too lenient with him."

Evie walked around the drawing room looking for a strategic place close to Tom. "You seem to think I chastised him and that's not the case."

"Oh, and that reminds me." Henrietta bounced on her chair and shifted to the edge. "Did you happen to send Barclay Chides a letter too? He seems to have disappeared. If you're not responsible, I think you might need to look into it. Something might have happened to him. For all we know, he could be lying in a ditch taking his last breath."

"I'm sure he's buried in a library somewhere looking up someone's family history." Evie looked at Tom for assistance. Usually, when she found herself in a tight spot, he came to her rescue. But he appeared to be preoccupied with the visitors book again. "What are you searching for?"

He closed the book and sat back. "I've been trying to find a connection between Lord Bertram and the people who visited the lodge at the same time. I was rather hoping to see Mr. Carter's name but I haven't found it. As a regular visitor, I assumed he would have accompanied Lord Bertram everywhere."

"I suppose the detective will want to get some facts from him and Mr. Carter will have to convince the detective he spent quite some time deciding what to do. He blames lethargy for his delay in coming down. Like us, he wasn't able to identify where the screams came from. But, unlike us, he didn't take quick action."

Henrietta looked eager to join in the conversation. "Tom's been telling us Mr. Carter and Mr. Bowles were both upstairs. The detective should place both men under arrest until one of them confesses. One or the other must be hiding something. Yes, indeed. One of them must have done it."

"Should the detective also subject them to some sort of torture?" Sara asked, her tone mocking.

Instead of answering, Henrietta looked over her shoulder and demanded, "Where is Edgar with the tea?"

"Oh, heavens." Evie gaped at Tom. "I just remembered. Earlier, we asked Edgar for tea and before he could bring it in, we left without saying anything to him."

Henrietta exchanged a sheepish look with Sara. "I'm afraid we also left him holding the tea tray. Do you think he is now trying to teach us a lesson? Perhaps he's taken a leaf from your book."

"What is that supposed to mean?" Evie asked.

"Well, you seem to be intent on putting everyone in their place. I think we should all apologize to Edgar before it's too late and he withholds our dinner."

Edgar startled everyone when he entered the drawing room and cleared his throat. "The detective has arrived and says he is here at your invitation, my lady."

"Yes, that's right, Edgar." Belatedly, Evie realized she hadn't informed Edgar. "My apologies, I should have mentioned it earlier."

Edgar inclined his head. "I will make the necessary arrangements, my lady."

Henrietta gave him her brightest smile. "You are an angel, Edgar. I don't know what we would ever do without you. I shall put in a good word for you and press her ladyship to give you a raise. You are worth your weight in gold."

When Edgar stepped out, Henrietta said, "I believe that will set his mind at ease. I always think you should make those around you feel valued."

Tom smiled at Evie and whispered, "I believe that is

your cue to make Henrietta feel valued. You should do it before she gives away your entire fortune."

Looking around, Evie asked, "Where's Toodles?"

"She's still in a strange mood. She mentioned something about going for a walk with Mr. Miller." Henrietta's eyes widened. "Oh, I think she might have wanted to send us a message. Although, what that might be I have no idea. I've come to realize I am no expert when it comes to reading between the lines. Then again, I suspect..."

When Henrietta broke off, Sara asked, "Suspect what?"

"That she prefers Mr. Miller's company to ours, of course."

"You might be right and I wouldn't blame her for being quite fed up with you."

"But you're the one who told her she had overstayed her welcome."

"I said no such thing."

This time, Tom whispered, "The border is nearby. Should we make a run for it?"

"I am tempted." All her efforts to bring order to her house had been for naught. It seemed they had all forgotten to leave their bickering behind. Catching a movement from the corner of her eye, she looked toward the door.

Caro stood there holding Holmes.

"Oh, heavens. Did I forget him again?"

Caro set him down and the little darling scampered straight toward Evie. She lifted him up and gave him her full attention with murmured assurances.

The conversation around her faded and she found herself thinking about eccentric behavior.

They had assumed Lord Bertram had been changed during the war, becoming quite odd and even talking to trees.

People's behavior could change over a long period of time as well as overnight, as she had recently witnessed.

She had come to assume there had been something in the air at Halton House affecting everyone and making them behave out of character.

She knew Henrietta had her moments of eccentricity, a tactic she seemed to employ in order to lighten the mood or change the subject.

If she really thought about it, there had always been a hint of eccentricity in Henrietta's behavior.

Mr. Roland Carter had known his lordship for a long time. Would his observations match everything Alice Brown had told them about Lord Bertram's behavior?

She only had a vague memory of him from his days of visiting the hunting lodge and she didn't feel she had known him well enough to now assist in sketching out his character.

While Alice Brown had told them his behavior had altered, they really had no way of knowing if this had been deliberate or a natural progression of age.

What if Lord Bertram had been trying to fool

everyone? She had already considered the possibility. But why would he want everyone to think he wasn't quite himself?

To hide his real intentions?

Which had been… What?

If they could somehow prove he had been quite deliberate in his attempt to mislead everyone, then they could focus on the reasons why he had taken such steps.

Holmes pressed his little nose against her chin, scattering all her thoughts and making her smile.

"I think it is safe to assume we will not be getting any tea today," Henrietta said.

CHAPTER 15

The drawing room
A few moments later...

The detective walked in and greeted everyone. "Well, it's official. My colleague is still working a case so I will be taking over the investigation and since you were both at the scene I have requested you both act as consultants."

Evie and Tom were lost for words. Especially Evie who was still reeling over what she considered to be the detective's deliberate evasiveness. Even after reasoning her way to seeing Tom's point of view, she felt the detective had a lot to answer for.

Henrietta stammered, "Detective, if your intention was to make an entrance, you succeeded brilliantly." She glanced at Sara. "But what about us? Are we included as consultants? Or are we expected to persuade you into enlisting our help by pointing out how instrumentally helpful we have been in the past?"

Still surprised by the detective's invitation, Evie suggested, "You and Sara can be our eyes and ears and since we're not dressing for dinner, we could start now. You might have noticed something that could help the case. What do we know so far?"

Henrietta bounced on her chair, her eyes brimming with excitement. "We know Lord Bertram is dead."

Sara frowned at her. "How does stating the obvious help?"

Looking confused, Henrietta said, "We are establishing what we know. Sometimes, the simplest methods are the most effective ones."

Sara didn't look convinced. "I'm sure Evie meant for us to think of something we might have missed. Something obscure. Something that might seem to be irrelevant but is, in fact, quite pertinent."

Everyone waited for Henrietta's reply. She took her time, in the process appearing to entertain several private thoughts which seemed to amuse her. Finally, she said, "I don't recall Evangeline asking me to read between the lines. We already know that is not my strength." Turning to Evie, she asked, "Is that what you meant?"

Giving Henrietta an encouraging smile, Evie suggested, "Perhaps the detective can start us off."

The detective leaned forward and clasped his hands. "Well, as a matter of fact, since Lady Henrietta—"

"Aha! I knew it. The finger of suspicion is being pointed at me."

"Henrietta, the detective is doing no such thing," Sara rebuked. "And you didn't let him finish."

They all gave him their full attention.

The detective pressed on, "Well, I was also going to mention Lady Sara and Toodles."

"Aha! So the three of us are under suspicion." Henrietta surged to her feet. Steadying herself, she lifted her chin and declared, "Toodles isn't here to defend herself, but I can assure you *she* had nothing to do with Lord Bertram's death."

"Henrietta!" Sara shifted to the edge of her seat. "You just suggested *we* had something to do with it."

"How on earth did you reach that conclusion? I never insinuate. I make statements. So you can't possibly have read anything between *my* lines, because there is nothing there. I can assure you, the space between my lines is quite devoid of meaning, undertone or insinuation. By all means, search for something, but you will find nothing."

Evie smiled. It was all she could do. She told herself she could learn to live with the lunacy. Somehow, everyone's behavior had been altered and she wondered if perhaps she needed to embrace it all and accept it not just as a temporary phase but, rather, as a permanent fixture in her household. Indeed, in her life.

Embracing her fate, Evie tried to steer the conversation in the right direction. "Henrietta, earlier you said you'd asked Lord Bertram about his predecessor and that prompted him to search for either a journal or a photograph."

Henrietta struck up an imperious pose. "Yes, that is correct. But I refuse to believe my curiosity sent him to his death."

Evie didn't want to tell her she had just read between the lines and found something that had not been there. She turned to look at the detective. "I believe that is a starting point. The journal or photograph might or might not be of significance."

Evie thought they now had a possible theory to work with. "The idea of searching for those items might have affected his lordship's behavior. In the process of trying to remember their whereabouts, he might have become confused. Remember the front door had been open, suggesting he might have been in the process of going out."

Tom agreed. "There is a long distance between that front door and the roof. Whatever happened to set him off had to be quite significant, something bad enough to distract and confuse him, muddling his thoughts to such an extent he didn't know if he was coming or going."

Henrietta exclaimed, "Are we still assuming he jumped to his death?"

"We are merely considering the possibility." Evie tried to picture Lord Bertram walking out of the library and heading to the front door. Why did he change his mind? Did he simply realize he'd been headed in the wrong direction? Or had he actually meant to head for the front door? "Heavens. The front door and the roof have one aspect in common."

"They are both exits," Tom said. "One more final than the other."

Henrietta didn't look convinced. "He might have made a mistake and then another and another. What if we are reading too much into his actions? It's possible he acted without any clear intention. Or… or he simply became bewildered."

"But what if confusion had nothing to do with it?" Tom then suggested playing with the idea of deliberate intention.

"In that case," Evie rose to her feet, "I wonder if we can assume the journal or the photograph posed some sort of problem or even a threat?"

"A threat?" Henrietta's eyes widened. "What sort of threat?"

"Evie doesn't know that yet," Sara said, her voice soothing. "Let her continue."

Evie picked up her thread of thought. "He considered making a run for it and then realized he needed something more final. Think about it. Why would someone throw themselves off a roof? Because they have been backed into a corner and they don't see a way out."

Sara and Henrietta looked shocked while the detective looked pensive.

Evie paced around the room and then stopped. "Henrietta, you asked him about his predecessor."

"Yes, and now I'm sorry I did."

"I think it might help to find out all we can about the previous Lord Bertram. Henrietta, I think I've asked you about him before. What do you remember about him?"

Henrietta closed her eyes for a moment. When she opened them, she spoke with absolute certainty. "He died."

Sara rolled her eyes. "I see you are sticking to facts."

"Do you remember how and where he died?" Evie asked.

Tom reached for the visitors book. After turning several pages, something caught his attention at the same time as Henrietta startled everyone by declaring, "Nineteen hundred and one."

Tom tapped his finger on the page. "Yes, that is about the time the handwriting changes."

Meaning, one Lord Bertram had died and another one had inherited the title.

Henrietta sat down and, shifting with restlessness, she turned to the detective and demanded, "Did you interrogate Mr. Carter and Mr. Bowles?"

"Yes, my lady. I questioned them." He confirmed what Evie already knew. They had both been upstairs.

"Surely, that places them both in a strategic position." Henrietta's gaze bounced from one to the other as if seeking support.

"Yes, my lady, but at this point, we would need some hard evidence or, indeed, a strong motivation. I believe her ladyship is correct in suggesting we should find out more about the previous Lord Bertram and focus on the journal and photograph. As I said, evidence or motivation is what is needed here…"

Henrietta's arms spread out like an operatic diva about to perform an aria. "One is the heir and the other… well, Mr. Carter must have a reason. He looks shifty. As soon as we arrived, he excused himself. What do you make of that? I think he wished to position himself in readiness for the attack."

Sara looked at Henrietta as if studying a curious object. "You assume he expected Lord Bertram to go up the stairs? Or do you think he ambushed him as he came out of the library and then dragged him up the stairs and onto the roof?"

"I obviously don't know the details, but I believe it's a sound theory worth pursuing." Henrietta clicked her fingers. "We should ring for some paper and write all this down. Evangeline has been known to do that. It's an effective method to keep track of suspects."

Evie looked at Tom and wondered if they should mention seeing Mr. Carter at the auction.

"Motive," Sara pointed out. "Mr. Carter would need a strong reason to commit such an atrocity."

Henrietta scoffed at the idea. "Not everyone needs a reason to justify their actions. Take Evangeline. I still do not understand why she felt compelled to write those letters so I'm inclined to think she didn't have a reason. And before you object, let me remind you, you were convinced she didn't have a reason."

"Other than wanting to get away from us," Sara murmured under her breath.

"What about the heir?" Henrietta asked as she spotted a small bell on a piecrust table and rang it. "Maybe he became tired of waiting for Lord Bertram to expire. You must agree, wanting to become the next Lord Bertram gives him a motive."

The detective sat back and stared at the fireplace. "I can't imagine Nigel Bowles risking his freedom to gain the title. It would simply be too foolish."

Tom remembered to mention what he'd found in his lordship's motor car. "Either Lord Bertram had been preparing to make a quick getaway or he had become quite eccentric, storing objects in the most unlikely places."

The information intrigued the detective. "I will want to speak to his lordship's physician to establish his state of mind."

"That won't be possible," Tom said. "According to Alice Brown, the doctor retired and has moved away."

The detective searched through his notebook. Putting it away, he checked his watch. "I'm afraid I must dash."

Evie swung toward him and frowned. She really needed to speak with him and clear the air once and for all before the issue became a comedy of errors.

As he stood up, he explained, "Mr. Carter and Mr. Bowles are both staying at Lynchfield Manor and I can't risk the journal and photograph going missing." He turned only to stop. "Oh, I almost forgot. Lady Woodridge, you were quite right about his lordship's fingers. There were traces of soot on his fingertips and moss under his fingernails." He looked down at the floor for a moment before adding, "Also, the back of his leg had a scrape." Without offering further explanations, he left.

As the door closed behind him, Henrietta looked from one to the other before saying, "Now that he's gone, we should get to work with our own investigation."

Edgar appeared and when Henrietta asked him for some paper, he looked completely nonplussed.

"It's quite safe," Henrietta assured him. "Her ladyship is not going to write any more letters. At least, I hope she won't."

CHAPTER 16

The tale is embroidered

So much had happened in only a short span of time, it took a moment for Evie to settle and quiet her mind. Out of everything they had talked about, the detective's parting comment demanded her attention.

How could he have delivered such news and then left without explaining what it meant?

Evie found herself understanding Henrietta's constant state of puzzlement and frustration.

"What is the matter?" Henrietta demanded. "You both look ghastly."

"Good heavens, Henrietta. Surely that is an exaggeration." Sara shook her head and assured them, "You both look lost for words. I'm sure that's what Henrietta meant to say."

Henrietta clucked her tongue. "And I'm sure I meant what I said. You should go out for a walk and clear your heads."

In the dark?

"Or perhaps you should try sharing your thoughts," Henrietta suggested.

Evie straightened in her chair. "I've been thinking about the scrape on the back of Lord Bertram's leg."

Tom stretched out and crossed his feet. "I've been thinking of nothing else for the last few minutes. Lord Bertram could have acquired that scrape at any time. He might have scraped his leg on the ledge as he lost his balance and fell or as someone pushed him. Or he might have injured himself in his library while trying to free himself from one of his chairs."

"I assume there are ways of determining how he got the scratch. Actually, there must be a more precise way of finding out."

"Yes, indeed," Tom agreed. "The height of the scratch could be measured against the height of the parapet and I'm sure the detective has already done that."

Evie felt the detective had been quite insensitive and wicked to have left them with this puzzle. How could he deliver such news and then leave them to deal with the mystery? "Do you suppose he is now convinced there is much more to his lordship's death?" With everything going on around her, Evie felt she needed some clarification. "That scrape on his leg has to mean someone pushed him and we know of two people who were upstairs at the time."

Henrietta drew their attention by waving a pen. "Before we continue to jump to conclusions about the heir, Nigel Bowles, could we please remember the two previous Lord Bertrams died under suspicious circumstances?"

One by one, they looked at Henrietta.

"I see, you are all surprised." Henrietta gave a sage nod. "You didn't think me capable of such clear thinking. I can't begin to tell you how satisfying it is to draw such attention at my age. Dare I hope, some of you might now hold a smidgen of admiration?"

"Henrietta, your opinions are always valued. We need to write it down as this is something definitely worth pursuing."

"Did you hear that, Sara?"

"I would write it all down for posterity but Edgar hasn't brought the paper or a pen yet," Sara complained.

"Henrietta, you said the previous Lord Bertram had died in nineteen hundred and one, but you didn't mention anything about his death being suspicious," Evie observed.

"I seem to recall there had been some sort of mystery behind it. I'm sure it will come to me." Satisfied, Henrietta stood up and walked around the drawing room murmuring to herself, "Inspiration struck once, it will strike again."

Henrietta had truly been inspired and the idea needed to be considered, right along with the others.

The fact Roland Carter and Nigel Bowles were both staying at the manor house worried Evie. The photograph and the journal could potentially provide a lead or even proof of wrongdoing. And they'd both had ample time to dispose of them.

Evie's eyes widened slightly. "That hadn't occurred to me." She hoped the detective arrived in time to find what could potentially turn out to be vital information.

"Are we supposed to guess?" Henrietta asked.

"I just thought of another possibility. Roland Carter and Nigel Bowles could be in league..."

Tom nodded. "We know Roland Carter is an opportunist."

"How do we know that?" Henrietta asked.

He explained about the auction they had attended. "He purchased a racehorse for next to nothing."

"Perhaps that's all it was worth," Henrietta suggested.

Tom's eyebrows dropped down as he spoke through gritted teeth, "It placed in the Grand National."

Henrietta's eyes widened. "Oh, heavens. Tom, you should have purchased it. Such an opportunity. How could you let it slip by?"

Tom glanced at Evie. "Indeed, but I wasn't allowed to bid on it."

As Henrietta offered her sympathies, Evie spun around and fixed her gaze on the fireplace. When they'd met Alice Brown, they hadn't considered the possibility that Lord Bertram's life could be in danger. Indeed, after leaving Lynchfield Manor, they had mostly been preoccupied with what they would face back at the hunting lodge.

They had only returned to Lynchfield Manor because Henrietta and the others had gone there and Evie had worried she might have been too hasty in deciding there had been no danger.

She thought about the significance of the timing. Why had Lord Bertram died just as they had arrived?

Keeping that thought in mind, she tried to piece together the sequence of events.

Assuming Lord Bertram had been killed, had someone wanted to take advantage of their presence so they could serve as witnesses or had their timely arrival been pure coincidence?

And if Lord Bertram had died by his own hands, why had he decided to kill himself when he had guests? It seemed more than likely that Lord Bertram had been disturbed by something.

In her mind, she saw him stepping out of the library and suddenly recognizing his mistake in agreeing to hunt down the photograph and journal.

Evie groaned with frustration. They had only discovered a few facts. The rest, they could only imagine.

Although...

She turned around and looked at Sara and Henrietta.

"Brace yourself, Sara. Evangeline is about to question us."

Evie nodded. "Do either of you remember exactly what happened when you arrived at Lynchfield Manor?"

Sara shifted to the edge of her chair. "When Lord Bertram opened the door, he looked stunned by the sight of us. As I said earlier, we had been arguing. I can't begin to imagine what he must have thought of us."

Henrietta brightened. "And then I saved the day by forging ahead. He recognized me and declared I was the real Countess of Woodridge." Henrietta nodded. "We then walked inside and I remember noticing the collection of swords on display."

"Who closed the door?" Evie asked.

Henrietta and Sara looked at each other. After a long moment, they both said, "Toodles."

Henrietta nodded. "Yes, it's coming back to me now. I remember hearing Toodles grumble about it. Then again, she grumbled all the way from Halton House. I do hope it's not a family trait."

"How sure are you that Toodles closed the door?"

"Oh, I have no doubt. As I said, she grumbled."

The door to the drawing room opened and Edgar walked in carrying a tray. It took everyone a few moments to remember he had been asked to bring some paper and a pen.

When he withdrew, Henrietta whispered, "He is determined to withhold our tea privileges."

Still engrossed with the idea of Roland Carter and Nigel Bowles banding together to do away with Lord Bertram, Evie tried to imagine what they stood to gain, other than the obvious. One would have the title and the house while the other might gain a favor.

She played around with the idea and then decided the detective had made a valid point. Nigel Bowles would be foolish to risk spending his life in prison.

Something else bothered her. The annoying timing of Nigel Bowles' visit. Yet another coincidence. Why had he decided to visit Lord Bertram now?

"Time is of the essence," Henrietta declared as she handed the paper to Sara. "We must ferret out some vital information before the detective beats us to it. That way, we shall prove our worth."

Evie crossed the room and sat down opposite her. "What do you remember about the previous Lord Bertram?"

"Why do you want to know about him?"

"I'm trying to form a picture." She sighed. "Actually, I'm trying to step back and distract myself."

Henrietta sat back and mused, "He enjoyed shooting. I remember seeing him in town once. He'd gone up to deal with some sort of legal matter and he'd dressed in his hunting tweeds instead of a suit suitable for a visit to town." Henrietta's eyes widened. "Oh, I remember now. 1901. Queen Victoria died."

As no one appeared to share her excitement, she went on to explain, "The previous Lord Bertram died in 1901. I've already mentioned that but I've now remembered something significant. Queen Victoria had a great fascination and passion for India. Of course, as you know, she was the Empress of India. Anyhow, that suddenly reminded me of a trip Lord Bertram made that year to India. That is where he died and the photo Julius, Lord Bertram, was going to look for was from that journey to India." She clicked her fingers. "When we arrived, I noticed the talwars and that's why I asked about the journey."

"Talwars? What are they?" Evie asked.

"They are Indian curved sabers. Anyhow, that's what triggered my curiosity about Alexander's journey."

"Alexander?" Evie parroted.

"The previous Lord Bertram. It's odd. I always knew him as Bertram but now that we are talking about two of them, I suppose it will become confusing."

"Do you happen to know how he died?"

"Oh, yes. It's come back to me." Henrietta shivered. "A hunting accident. He was one of the best shots around. It seems ironic that he should have been killed by someone who couldn't handle a gun." Henrietta gave a slow shake of her head. "Yes, yes. It's all coming back to me now. It took some time for the news to reach England."

"What happened to the person responsible for his death?" Evie asked.

Henrietta shrugged. "I have no idea. I only ever heard the death referred to as an accident." Henrietta's gaze drifted to the door.

Edgar stood there giving everyone the impression he had been there for some time. Eventually, he announced, "Dinner is served."

Lowering her voice, Henrietta whispered, "I suppose that makes it official. We will not be having tea today. Of course, there is no question of delaying dinner until the detective returns. It would be too risky to test Edgar's patience. We might all end up having to acquire cooking skills."

"Thank you, Edgar," Evie said. "We will be along shortly."

Edgar did not move.

Leaning in, Henrietta whispered, "I believe he intends to make sure we all make our way to the dining room."

CHAPTER 17

The next morning

The detective helped himself to some eggs and sat down. After taking a bite of his toast, he looked up and saw all eyes were on him. Without being prompted, he knew everyone had been waiting to hear news about his investigation, especially as they had all assumed he had returned to Lynchfield Manor. "We searched every nook and cranny in that house and found absolutely nothing. Not a single photograph or journal."

"In other words," Henrietta said, "you were too late. The culprit has taken the evidence. However, not all is lost as the absence of those items can only mean they hold the key to Lord Bertram's death. Otherwise, why would they go missing?" Henrietta clapped. "Oh, heavens. I believe I am still inspired."

Sara took a sip of her tea and murmured, "Don't let it go to your head, Henrietta."

"Did you search the motor car?" Tom asked.

"From top to bottom. I questioned Nigel Bowles and he couldn't explain why Lord Bertram had stowed the paintings and silver in the motor."

Tom drained his cup of coffee and sat back. "I also saw a suitcase and that's why I assumed he had been preparing for a journey or even planning to escape. Did you find clothing or something else inside?"

"Suitcase?" The detective shook his head. "No, I didn't find a suitcase." He retrieved his notebook and made a note of it.

Henrietta looked startled. "Did I miss something? Does this mean someone took the suitcase?"

"It would appear so, my lady. While we did a thorough search of the house, we were not specifically looking for a suitcase. Regardless, we did come across several of them in the house, but they were all empty."

"Am I writing this down?" Sara asked.

"Yes, please do." Henrietta took a quick sip of her tea. "I hope you find this odd, detective. Someone didn't care enough about the paintings and silver but they absconded with the suitcase. Surely that means it contained something other than clothing."

"Most likely, my lady."

"But, where will you search for it? And does this suggest someone did, in fact, kill Lord Bertram? Or did someone merely take advantage of his death." Henrietta didn't give the detective a chance to reply. "Oh, my goodness. This has to mean the suitcase contained something quite valuable. We might even be on the right track about the journal and photograph. I wonder if, when we do find the items, we'll even know what to look for."

They were all impressed by Henrietta's reasoning.

This certainly increased the significance of those items.

As the detective made another note in his book, Evie thought about the suitcase's disappearance.

Tom had seen it earlier that day. Had it been taken before or straight after Lord Bertram's death, while the detective had been talking to Alice Brown or afterwards, when everyone had returned to the hunting lodge?

"This is going to be a long day," Henrietta complained. "I trust you will continue with your investigation. Meanwhile, we will all be sitting here waiting for news." Looking at Evie, she added, "I suppose you two will also be setting out."

"I hadn't really given it any thought, Henrietta. However, I had been wanting to follow up on something."

"Well, do share. Otherwise, I'll be on edge all day."

"It's not really connected to Lord Bertram's death. At least, I don't think it is. I'm only curious about the auction we attended. It all seems rather odd and I wish to get some answers." Their outing would also serve the purpose of keeping her mind occupied with the continuing puzzle of the auction and away from thoughts about Caro and the detective, as well as Toodles who hadn't come down to breakfast.

"I can't speak for Toodles, but we will, of course, remain here and stay out of everyone's way," Henrietta declared. "It might take me all day to decipher Sara's scribblings, but I will also turn my thoughts to everything we know in an effort to identify anything that might be of use."

Tom looked down at Evie's lap. "Have you forgotten someone this morning?"

Evie smiled. "Certainly not. Holmes is on the floor nibbling my shoe laces."

"Are you sure?" Tom asked.

Hesitating, Evie glanced down but didn't see Holmes. Where had the little scamp disappeared to? "I swear he was there a moment ago."

Hearing Edgar clearing his throat, Evie turned and saw him standing by the sideboard... with Holmes curled up in his arms. "I caught Master Holmes chewing on *my* shoelaces, my lady."

Evie read between the lines and noted Edgar's hint of disapproval. Setting her cup down, she gestured with her hands. "Hand him over, please. I promise I will not let him out of my sight."

After breakfast, Evie rushed upstairs to fetch her coat. "You really should try to stay on Edgar's good side and please, don't ever chew on his shoelaces again."

To her surprise, she didn't find Caro or Millicent in her room and just as well because she didn't want any delays. She and Tom needed to set off as soon as possible.

The auction had taken place only a couple of days before. For all she knew, the Guilfords might have already packed up and left for London.

Setting Holmes down on the bed, she put on her coat and adjusted a hat in place.

"Ned Brixton," she murmured. The groundskeeper might have seen someone taking off with the suitcase. Indeed, he might have taken it himself.

Between the time Tom had discovered the suitcase in the car and the time the detective returned to Lynchfield Manor, the window of opportunity had been there for the taking.

She hoped all the activity at Lynchfield Manor had aroused the neighbor's curiosity, enough for them to be quite alert and remain vigilant.

Casting a quick glance at her reflection, she swung around and rushed out of the bedroom. A second later, she rushed back in and scooped Holmes off the bed.

Tom stood at the bottom of the stairs waiting for her. "You forgot him again."

"How could you possible tell?"

"Guilt is written all over your face. Your eyes tend to widen slightly and your eyebrows curve up."

Evie scowled. "Do I need to remind you we are trying to make sense of an unexpected death? I can't think of everything." She looked toward the dining room. "Is the detective still here?"

"No, he just left."

"Oh, I wanted to remind him about Ned Brixton. He might have seen something. Never mind, I'm sure the detective will be speaking with the neighbors at some point."

Tom held the front door open for her and they made their way to the roadster. "Have you come up with a plan? How are we going to approach the Guildfords?"

"We might need to be honest. Otherwise, it will take too much effort to work our curiosity into the conversation."

"You're not worried they will refuse to talk about a subject that has clearly caused them pain?"

"I think it might be a case of the end justifying the means. Roland Carter purchased a valuable horse for next to nothing and the more I think about it the more convinced I am there was something underhanded about the deal. Also, there might be a connection to Lord Bertram's death, albeit a flimsy one. I've been trying to ignore the thought but it refuses to go away. It can't hurt to snoop around."

As they wound their way out of the hunting lodge estate and onto the main road, Evie tried to organize her thoughts.

Sooner or later, Henrietta would realize she might

have been, in a roundabout way, instrumental in Lord Bertram's demise. If they were indeed on the right track, mentioning the journal and photograph had sent him to his death.

She knew Henrietta could be pragmatic and wouldn't blame herself. In case she did, she'd have to be ready to talk sense into her.

Examining her thoughts, Evie wondered if there had been more to the conversation. Henrietta must have said something else, something quite fatal.

"I wonder if the newspapers reported the death of the previous Lord Bertram? They must have. It will help to know as much as we can about his death. Henrietta's observation about both Lord Bertrams dying under suspicious circumstances is worth delving into."

Where would they find archival copies of newspapers from 1901?

When they neared the village, Evie pointed ahead. "Please stop in the village. I need to send a telegram."

When Tom stopped the motor, she explained, "I think it's time we involve Lotte. She will know how to research the newspapers in an expedient manner."

Evie handed Holmes over to him and rushed across the street. At the postal office, she composed a message. Reading it, she glanced up from the piece of paper and looked at the young woman standing behind the counter. Fearing word would spread about her involvement in the investigation, she couldn't risk spelling out her request in the message to Lotte.

Evie folded the piece of paper, tucked it in her pocket and wrote another message.

Urgent information needed regarding predecessor's demise. Anything printed 01.

She couldn't tell if it sounded too cryptic. However, she decided to trust Lotte's ability to decipher the message.

Since time remained of the essence, it would have to do until she returned to the hunting lodge. She'd then be able to place a telephone call and make sure she had set Lotte on the right path.

Satisfied with the message she had written, she handed the piece of paper to the young woman and payed for the telegram.

Outside, she found Tom chatting with someone who looked familiar. As Evie approached the roadster, they ended their conversation and the woman strolled away.

"That was Holmes' previous owner. She wanted to know how he was settling in."

"I hope you lied through your teeth."

"Ah, there's that guilt again." He lifted Holmes up and looked at him. "He appears to be quite content with his new situation. In any case, he's still young and will no doubt soon forget his rocky start in your household."

"If only you'd found a hound dog. He might have been able to lead us to the suitcase."

They were back on the road when Tom said, "I hope the detective inspected the area surrounding the motor car. There might be some sort of trace of the suitcase being dragged away."

"Surely a strong man would have no trouble lifting it and carrying it." A moment later, she exclaimed, "Oh. We're assuming a man took the suitcase."

"Yes, indeed. It might have been a woman."

Someone working at the house or someone else?

Evie drew in a long breath. Had the journal been hidden inside the suitcase and what significance did it hold? At the moment, that remained their main concern.

"Whose journal is it?" she found herself asking.

"Pardon?"

"Are we looking for Julius' journal or Alexander's journal?"

Tom slowed down, suggesting his thoughts had been engaged.

The detective's search had been thorough and he had found no other journal in the house. Otherwise, he would have mentioned it. If someone kept a journal, they would surely have filled several of them over time.

Tom tapped his finger on the steering wheel. "Since Henrietta asked about the previous Lord Bertram, I assume it belonged to him."

Evie agreed, saying, "Alexander Bertram's personal possessions must have been sent back to England after his death in 1901."

What were they missing?

Evie felt they had key pieces of a puzzle but had no idea how to put them together.

Once again, she went through the process of picturing Lord Bertram stepping out of the library and going in search of the journal only to realize…

What had he realized?

That the journal contained some sort of vital information about his predecessor's death and he couldn't risk anyone else finding out about it?

Heavens. That would be a cause for concern if he'd had something to do with his death.

What other information could have set Lord Bertram on a path to destruction?

Julius Bertram hadn't been a direct heir. Perhaps there had been something about the line of succession. Evie's thoughts stalled for a moment. In a death such as this one, one would inevitably look at the heir for answers which, in this case, happened to be Nigel Bowles. Could one do the same with Lord Bertram's predecessor? What if Julius Bertram had been involved in getting rid of Alexander Bertram back in 1901? Fear of discovery and the consequences that would follow might have sent him rushing up to the roof.

A moment later, she remembered the scrape on the back of his leg. This suggested he had been killed. Or did it?

"You're frowning," Tom said.

"I'm about to begin tearing my hair out. I keep thinking about the journal containing something vital. What if the information it contains affected more than one person and Lord Bertram was killed because of it?"

She could feel her shoulders tensing with frustration. "We are nowhere near that wonderful process of elimination where we can narrow our theories and point the finger at one specific person."

"Are you now gritting your teeth?" Tom asked.

"I'm close to it. And I fear I'm going to stroke Holmes' fur right off him." She looked down at Holmes and gave him an apologetic smile. "The person who took the suitcase did so knowing it contained the journal. I'm almost certain of it. But why take the whole suitcase? Why not just retrieve the journal?"

Tom laughed. Leaning in, he said, "I hope you realize you'll have to remember all these questions and repeat them so Sara can write everything down. Actually, once Henrietta finds out how much theorizing she's missing out on, she will insist on coming along with us next time we trek out."

She looked at her watch and wondered if Lotte had already begun her search for information. Knowing Lotte had her own case to focus on, Evie knew she needed to be patient. With so many questions floating around her mind, they also needed to start getting some answers.

She closed her eyes and tried to quieten her mind. Focusing on the roar of the engine only made her think of their arrival at the Guildford house and the fact they didn't have a plan. Would Mr. and Mrs. Guildford want to talk about the fact they'd sold their precious possessions including a racehorse that might have gone on to win the Grand National? She didn't think so.

Abandoning her efforts to quieten her mind, she

asked, "Do you think we would be treading on toes if we asked to look around Lynchfield Manor?"

Tom grinned. "I doubt it. Remember, the detective appreciates our observant eyes."

Belatedly, she wished they had remained at Lynchfield Manor to have a proper look around, but they had all been in shock and she had been reluctant to impose on the detective's investigation.

Evie closed her eyes again and made another attempt to quieten her mind.

Two long breaths into her meditation and she opened her eyes again.

"I wonder when the funeral service will be held. It will give us an opportunity to observe the people attending." Evie gasped. Had there been someone else in the house?

If Lord Bertram hadn't fallen or jumped, someone had pushed Lord Bertram off the roof, either by force, by coercion, or even by fear. Then, during the chaos that had ensued as they'd rushed inside the house, the person might have fled.

Evie turned to Tom. "I think you need to stop. My head is spinning and I fear it is about to explode."

A moment later, they sat by the side of the road. Neither one spoke.

Dragging in a breath, Evie erupted from the motor car.

Tom sat back and watched Evie pacing in a tight circle. She stopped and gazed into the distance.

Deep down, Evie felt she might have been able to

prevent Lord Bertram's death. She had already admitted to feeling as though she had failed. Would Lord Bertram still be alive if they hadn't all trekked up here? She forced herself to dismiss the thought. However, she now accepted full responsibility.

Turning, she marched back and settled into the passenger's seat.

From the start, she had harbored suspicions about Mr. Carter. "I feel we should be methodical. We should focus on eliminating Mr. Carter as a suspect."

Tom put the motor car into gear and she thought she heard him say, "Isn't that what we were going to do all along?"

CHAPTER 18

*W*hen the Guildford house came into view, Tom glanced at Evie and gave her a reassuring smile while Evie replied with a firm nod. They were ready to tackle Mr. and Mrs. Guildford and wring out the information they needed from them.

Slowing down a fraction, Tom made the turn into the driveway just as another motor car blazed its way out of the estate.

It all happened in a flash and swerving out of the way nearly sent them into a ditch.

Once the mechanical sounds of the roadster coming to a sudden stop stilled, they both sat back. Tom's fingers released their hold on the steering wheel while Evie looked down at Holmes who remained impervious to the near miss. In fact, judging by the energetic wag of his tail, he'd found it rather exciting.

While the other motor raced away, Evie and Tom

took stock of the situation, both recognizing how close they had come to disaster.

Evie held Holmes against her chest, her breath rushing in and out until it finally steadied. At least she hadn't screamed.

Responding to Tom's look of concern, Evie said, "I'm fine and so is Holmes."

He nodded. "Follow that motor?"

"Yes. Yes, follow it."

The driver had been nothing but a blur. However, they had to assume they were following either Mr. or Mrs. Guildford.

After several minutes of driving, they caught sight of the motor car. Instead of catching up to it, Tom maintained a discreet distance, although it would be difficult to imagine anyone not realizing they were being followed since they were the only two motor cars on the narrow country road.

"The driver appears to be heading back to the village which should make it easier for us," Tom observed. "I suppose we will have to contrive a chance encounter."

A short while later, however, they experienced an unexpected stroke of good luck when the motor slowed down, swerving slightly before coming to a full stop.

"It looks like the driver has run into a spot of trouble." Tom grinned. "This is our chance."

The driver, a woman, emerged from the motor and

looked one way and then the other. Seeing them, she waved.

"It looks like it's Mrs. Guildford." Evie had hoped it would be the husband as the wife had come across as being more decisive, with a stronger will and firmness of purpose.

Still smiling, Tom said, "Finally, I think we have a strategy. I'll take care of the motor while you prod Mrs. Guildford for information."

"Sounds like a splendid scheme. I'm glad we were spared the ordeal of chasing her around the village. If that had, indeed, been her destination. Do you think we should be honest and tell her we had been on our way to see her?"

Tom brought the roadster to a stop and looked at her. "I'm guessing you have already considered several scenarios."

Evie nodded. "I've thought of several ways she might respond. Unfortunately, I'm relying on my observations of her so they are not all favorable."

Shaking his head, Tom said, "Sometimes, I think it must be exhausting being you."

"I suppose that means you are simply happy of this opportunity and haven't thought ahead. What if she baulks at the idea of sharing information with us?"

"You can employ your powers of persuasion."

"You seem to place a lot of trust in a talent I'm not sure I possess."

Mrs. Guildford approached the roadster. "I am so glad you came along. I don't know what I would have done if I'd had to deal with this by myself. My motor simply stopped without any warning."

Evie watched for any signs of recognition. After all, it had only been a couple of days since they had attended the auction and only a few minutes since she had nearly run them off the road. However, Mrs. Guildford simply looked relieved by the sight of them. Although, Evie thought that might change at any moment as recognition sometimes took a while to sink in.

Emerging from the roadster, Evie gave her a bright smile. "You're lucky we came along. Mr. Winchester knows all about motor cars. He'll have you back on the road in no time." After assuring her, she introduced herself and Tom.

"How do you do. I'm Mrs. Guildford."

As she still gave no indication of having seen them before, Evie had to decide which strategy would work best for her. A casual approach with a hint of curiosity might eventually yield results, but they only had a limited amount of time.

Leaving her to her own devices, Tom removed his coat and walked around the motor inspecting it for damages.

Mrs. Guildford pressed her hand to her chest. "Oh, dear. I do hope he can fix it."

"Motors are wonderful inventions," Evie said. "Unfortunately, they do require constant attention."

Mrs. Guildford spoke with a distracted tone, "Yes, indeed. We normally take good care of it but lately our minds have been preoccupied with other matters."

"Oh, I'm sorry to hear that. It shouldn't take long to fix, I'm sure." Evie gave her an apologetic smile. "This might not be the right moment to mention it, but we were actually on our way to see you."

Mrs. Guildford tore her attention away from her motor and glanced at Evie.

Evie explained how she and Tom had attended the auction. Unfortunately, this turned out to be a mistake.

"I see." Mrs. Guildford's lips pursed and she looked away.

Feeling she had just had a door slammed in her face, Evie explained, "We attended the auction out of sheer curiosity. You see, we suddenly found ourselves in the village and when we didn't see anyone about, we asked where all the locals were." She immediately sensed her honest revelation had failed to have the desired effect.

With her tone full of disapproval, Mrs. Guildford said, "Yes, many people came out of sheer curiosity."

Thinking the opportunity would slip through her fingers, she decided to play her sympathy card. "I couldn't help feeling distraught by the whole experience. I told Tom I couldn't imagine parting with such beautiful items. I realize they are only material objects but their absence would definitely create a void."

"As you said, they are only objects." Instead of softening toward her, Mrs. Guildford's stiff tone suggested she had no further interest in the subject.

"I must admit, I found myself particularly intrigued

by the sale of your racehorse," Evie continued.

At that precise moment, Mrs. Guildford tensed.

"I found it odd that you should sell it at a house auction instead of through Tattersalls. Specially as it has such an illustrious pedigree." She wasn't entirely sure if that had been the appropriate remark to make about a horse. Dogs had pedigrees. Horses, on the other hand, might require some other precise definition to cast light on their prowess.

Impatient, Mrs. Guildford took a step away as she clipped out, "It was a matter of expediency." She walked up to her motor car and asked Tom, "Can you see what's wrong with it?"

"Not yet."

Holmes snuggled against Evie and nibbled the edge of her collar. Determined to get the woman to talk, Evie walked toward Mrs. Guildford's motor and tried to think of another way to approach her.

Evie had tried to sound sympathetic. Would the woman respond to a more direct approach?

Evie went to stand next to her and looked at her watch.

Mrs. Guildford noticed this and apologized for keeping them. "I do hope you don't have to rush off somewhere."

Under any other circumstance, Evie would have offered assurances. However, she needed to press on. "Actually, Mr. Winchester and I are currently involved in an investigation."

The remark appeared to spur her interest. At least,

that's how Evie interpreted the woman's slightly raised eyebrow.

"I suppose you've heard about Lord Bertram's death."

Mrs. Guildford gave a small shake of her head. "Dreadful. Simply dreadful."

Sounding surprised, Evie asked. "Did you know him?"

"Only in passing."

"Well, the fact is, one of the guests staying at Lynchfield Manor attended your auction." Evie tested the waters by withholding the name. "We were curious to find out if you knew anything about him."

Tom continued inspecting the motor but he glanced up a couple of times to gage Mrs. Guildford's reaction.

"You say you're investigating the matter?" Mrs. Guildford asked. "In what capacity?"

"Mr. Winchester and I work for a lady's detective agency."

Tom's raised eyebrow caught Evie's attention. It took her a moment to realize he might not be entirely comfortable being associated with a lady's detective agency.

"We are also officially consulting with the police," Evie added.

"Really?"

Belatedly, Evie realized she had just informed a member of the public that the Countess of Woodridge had taken up a profession. So much for remaining incognito.

Giving her attention to Holmes, Evie said, "Of course, you might prefer to speak with the police..."

"The police?"

"Yes. This is an official investigation."

"Shouldn't you have a badge of sorts?"

Heavens. She didn't even have a business card. She would definitely need to do something about that.

"We don't need one. However, if you would like to confirm our involvement, feel free to contact Detective Evans. In any case, he will be more than happy for you to answer his questions at the local constabulary."

As hoped, Mrs. Guildford didn't care for the idea. She cringed with great displeasure. Although, despite her obvious reluctance to speak with the police at some gloomy office, she didn't exactly encourage Evie to ask her questions.

Regardless, Evie forged ahead. "Mr. Roland Carter has been a guest at Lynchfield Manor." Evie kept a close eye on her reaction and thought she saw Mrs. Guildford flinch. "We know he attended your auction. In fact, he purchased your horse."

"I see."

Evie had expected to see a more dramatic reaction. Then, she noticed Mrs. Guildford's cheeks had turned a deep shade of crimson. A sure sign she had reacted to Evie's remark.

At that moment, Evie knew there had to be a story behind the sale of the racehorse. Specifically, the purchase of the horse by Mr. Carter.

"I had the impression you didn't really want to sell

the horse."

"What are you accusing me of?" Mrs. Guildford spluttered. "This is utter nonsense."

Evie considered Mrs. Guildford's response. She had gone on the defensive. Also, her response hadn't exactly sounded like a denial.

Evie gave her a moment to calm down. But not too long. "This is precisely what the detective will want to know."

Mrs. Guildford dragged in a breath and straightened. "I fail to see how this could be relevant to your investigation."

"We are mapping out Mr. Carter's movements prior to Lord Bertram's death and, ultimately, we feel we will be able to define his motivation." Evie hoped she had sounded convincing. As she held Mrs. Guildford's gaze, she saw Tom, who stood just behind Mrs. Guildford, looking at her, his expression rather impressed.

"I'm afraid I can't help you with that information. We didn't make his acquaintance." Mrs. Guildford lifted her chin. "In fact, I barely noticed him."

"Not even when he purchased your valuable horse for next to nothing? I find that hard to believe." Evie brushed her finger under Holmes' chin. Suddenly, inspiration struck. "Were you coerced into selling the horse?"

Mrs. Guildford stepped away and waved.

Confused by her action, Evie turned and saw a motor car approaching. Clearly, Mrs. Guildford had decided to seek someone else's assistance.

CHAPTER 19

Nothing ventured, nothing gained

Tom and Evie stood by the side on the road watching Mrs. Guildford's motor car disappear into the distance.

The well-intentioned man who had stopped to assist tipped his hat, waved and drove off.

"Well, I guess that's that."

"You did your best, Countess. That's all you can ever do. And, I must say, your technique has much improved. You came very close to wrangling the information out of her by using fear. She is definitely hiding something."

"Yes, but is it at all relevant?"

Tom held the passenger door open for her. "I'm surprised you ask. In the past, you have entertained some wild theories which proved to be quite instrumental in identifying a culprit. Mrs. Guildford is most certainly withholding information and it might well be part of the puzzle."

Evie didn't understand why Mrs. Guildford would refuse to share something that could assist the police in identifying a possible suspect. She had to be hiding something huge. At least, that's what Evie imagined.

So far, no one had fallen under suspicion because there had been no clear evidence of involvement in a crime.

What did a real detective do in such a case?

"I would like to think she will talk with her husband and then change her mind and volunteer the information. And, now more than ever, I am convinced we are on the right track. There is some sort of connection here and we need to find it." She glanced at Tom. While he listened to her, he didn't give anything away. "I know you think this is mere coincidence, but if I'm right and Mr. Carter has a talent for coercion, then he might have applied it to Lord Bertram." Of course, until she found some sort of proof, the idea of him forcing the Guildford couple to sell their horse remained a supposition. Perhaps even a highly improbable one.

Regardless, in her opinion, the practice of observation had its merits. At worst, she would be proven wrong. She hoped that wouldn't be the case. Otherwise, what good would she be as a lady detective?

"Where are we headed now?" Tom asked. "Lynch-field Manor?"

"Yes, please. We might find the detective there."

Along the way, she thought about her inspired idea.

Had coercion played a role in the decision to sell the racehorse? She had no idea how or why it had occurred to her. Although, there had been that moment at the auction when Mr. Carter's expression had displayed such cruelty it had left a strong impression in her mind. And the Guildford couple had not looked pleased about parting with the horse. It almost made sense to imagine they had been forced into selling the horse.

"Oh."

"That sounds promising," Tom said.

"I do hope so. We could try to find the auctioneer. He might be prepared to tell us something."

"Such as?"

Evie smiled. "How the horse came to be included in the action. For all we know, it might have been a late addition."

"You're determined to connect Mr. Carter to some sort of wrongdoing."

"I am determined to leave no stone unturned."

Evie's spirits lifted and her mind cleared, allowing her to focus on the idea that had begun to take shape.

In order to employ coercion, one would need to have some sort of advantage, something which could be used to target the Guildford couple. Yes, some sort of leverage.

What did the Guildford couple value above all else?

They were selling a house which had been part of their heritage, right along with their valuable possessions. That told her they were practical and not at all nostalgic, relying on common sense rather than emotions.

Everyone valued their freedom. What would put it at risk for Mr. and Mrs. Guildford?

Lost in her thoughts, it took her a moment to notice they had arrived.

Tom leaned forward and glanced around the entrance to Lynchfield Manor. "I don't see the detective's motor."

"I'm actually grateful and relieved Edmonds isn't here. Henrietta said they would remain at the hunting lodge but I wouldn't be surprised if she decides to follow a hunch."

"What tactic will you employ this time?"

Humming, Evie tilted her head from side to side. "If anyone asks questions, we can proceed with confidence because we are working as consultants."

Instead of ringing the front door bell, they walked around to the back of the house and tried their luck there.

To their surprise, Alice Brown saw them walking by the kitchen window and met them at the back door.

"Alice, how are you? I'm surprised to see you here."

Alice wiped her hands on her apron. "I'm fine, milady. I thought it would be best to keep busy. Mr. Bowles and Mr. Carter are still here so someone needs to be at hand. Mrs. Forbes is about to arrive to prepare lunch for them."

"Was the cook here yesterday?"

"Yes, she prepared lunch and then left."

That would have been between their visit in the morning and Henrietta's visit in the afternoon. "Is that what she usually does?"

"Yes, Lord Bertram..." Alice took a deep swallow. "His lordship only had lunch, preferring something light in the evenings, usually leftovers from lunch which I always put together for him before I left for the day."

"Is the other housemaid here?"

Alice nodded. "June came but only because she knew I would be here. She keeps looking over her shoulder expecting to see his lordship's ghost hovering nearby."

"What about Mr. Carter? Has he kept you busy?"

"Not at all. He's been keeping to himself. In fact, he has barely come out of his room."

"And the heir?"

"Mr. Bowles is trying to sort out the mess in the library." Alice looked over her shoulder. "I should really start referring to him as his lordship."

Evie looked at Tom. "I suppose we should make our presence known to Mr. Bowles."

"His lordship," Tom corrected.

"Yes, of course."

"I'll prepare some tea and bring it in," Alice offered.

They made their way to the library, along the way

scrutinizing everything in their path. To Evie's amusement, Tom tapped a few walls.

"Do you expect to find a secret compartment?"

"You never know. Remember, we are still looking for the missing journal and photograph."

Evie nodded. "As well as the other journals. I'm sure there must be more."

They reached the library and found the new Viscount Bertram standing on a ladder putting a book in a shelf."

Seeing them, he stepped down. "Lady Woodridge and Mr. Winchester. What a surprise."

"Lord Bertram."

He raked his fingers through his hair. "Ah, yes. I suppose that is now the case. I doubt it will make much difference to me."

"How does your family feel about it?" The fact the title had gone to him indicated the absence of a father.

"My mother is probably going around telling all her neighbors. As excited as she must be, I doubt she'll ever bother to come up to see the house. She dislikes traveling."

He didn't mention a wife so she assumed he didn't have one.

He looked about the library and shrugged. "I've been hunting down books on animal husbandry. Someone has to take care of the pigs and since I won't have much else to do, it might as well be me."

For a moment, Evie thought she caught a hint of

Julius Bertram's odd behavior. "Oh, yes. The pigs must be taken care of."

"Do sit down. I'll ring for some tea."

"Alice Brown is already taking care of it. We saw her on our way in. Actually, we should apologize. Mr. Winchester and I were eager to see how she was faring. She had a dreadful experience yesterday. Anyhow, we went directly to the kitchen," Evie explained and walked about the room inspecting the books, many of which had already found their way into the shelves. Glancing at the new Lord Bertram, she wondered if he'd been looking for something…

The sound of a hard thud startled Evie. Everyone looked up.

"Good heavens," Evie exclaimed.

"That must be Mr. Carter. He's been poking around the attic."

"Perhaps we should go up to see if he needs assistance." Evie didn't wait for an answer. Walking out of the library, she glanced over her shoulder and saw the new Lord Bertram wasn't following them. Instead, he turned his attention back to the books.

Outside the library, Evie whispered, "Do you know which way we are going?"

"Up?"

"Yes, that would be my guess too."

Along the way, they kept an eye out for anyone who might help them find their way to the attic only to remember there were only two servants in the house.

Reaching the first floor, Evie looked up. "We know

these stairs lead to the roof. There must be another way up."

Tom gestured to the hallway. "Let's try this way."

Opening each door as they went along, they encountered one bedroom after another. When they found a narrow hallway, they followed it to the end. Opening the last door, they both nodded and went through. The stairs were easily identified as the ones used by servants because they lacked the sort of embellishments displayed throughout the rest of the house.

Just as they went up the first step, they saw the housemaid coming down, her steps hurried.

Evie smiled. "Jane. Hello."

"It's June, milady."

"My apologies. I'm simply dreadful with names. Mr. Winchester and I are trying to find the attic."

"These stairs will lead you up." She looked over her shoulder. "I... I heard a noise and went up to see. Mr. Carter is up there." Nodding, June hurried down and went through the door they had just come through.

"I find it interesting that she should happen to be nearby."

"Are you going to include June in your list of suspects?"

"You know very well I don't have one of those. It's been impossible to compile a list because we don't know enough about anyone. For instance, where did the new Lord Bertram live and what did he do? He is a distant relative and I assume he had a profession but he just said he now has nothing much to do. As for Mr. Carter, he has already attempted to maintain a cloak of mystery around himself so we know next to nothing about him."

"That's only because you were not able to trick him into revealing where he lives."

"I see. You are teasing me."

Tom grinned.

"I still find it difficult to tell. I suppose that means you are an expert at it."

"I have to be good at something."

Evie laughed. "And so you are happy to excel at teasing me."

Tom eased the door to the attic open and they both peered inside. Two lamps illuminated the area close to the door and they could see a light moving further ahead suggesting Mr. Carter was using a candle to light the way.

Evie called out a greeting.

"Lady Woodridge and Mr. Winchester. Fancy meeting you here," Roland Carter spoke as if distracted by something.

"We heard a sound and thought we should see if you needed assistance."

"I hope I didn't alarm Lord Bertram."

Tom and Evie edged their way through a maze of old furniture and trunks.

"We left him sorting out books."

"Oh, yes. He's taken up where Julius left off."

"That's an interesting way of putting it," Evie whispered to herself. Somewhere in the back of her mind, the remark triggered her suspicions and set wheels in motion.

If she wanted to make a success of being a lady detective, she would need to hone her skills and that included listening to what people said because they might give themselves away.

"I didn't expect to see you again, my lady."

"You're bound to see even more of us as we're consulting with Detective Evans."

That caught his attention.

"In fact, we have been busy today and have just been chatting with Mrs. Guildford." She stood close enough to him to see his reaction. Evie thought she saw him still for a moment, but he recovered and swung away to set a book down on a trunk.

"It's quite dusty in here and I'm afraid if I spend too long looking through the treasure chests I'll start sneezing."

"Have you been searching for something in particular?" Tom asked as they began making their way toward the door.

"Every house has its secrets, Mr. Winchester. One never knows what one will find. Every time I've visited, I've enjoyed spending time up here rummaging around. If you're interested in fashion, my lady, you'll find a wardrobe full of ladies' gowns dating back over a hundred years."

Evie pretended to be distracted by an interesting vase. "There is definitely an impressive hoard in here.

Perhaps Lord Bertram should consider holding an auction. Do you attend many of those?"

"Only if I happen to be in the area." He blew out the candle. "I certainly don't go hunting around for them."

As they left the attic and made their way down, Evie said, "Mrs. Guildford mentioned something about selling her racehorse."

"Did she?" He sounded surprised.

Deciding to bait him, she said, "Yes. She appeared to regret selling it."

"I'm sorry to hear that."

"Why is that?" she asked.

"Because I purchased it," he admitted.

Heavens. She hadn't expected him to come straight out and say it. "What will you do with the horse?"

"I must admit I haven't given it much thought."

Did that mean he had purchased it on a whim? It would derail her theory which had only now begun to take shape.

She still maintained the Guildford couple had been forced into selling it and, for that to happen, she thought they would need a strong reason.

What sort of information would someone like Mr. Carter use to force their hand?

When they reached the hall and turned toward the library, Evie said, "If you change your mind about owning a racehorse, Mr. Winchester will gladly take it off your hands."

"I doubt I will sell it anytime soon. It placed at the Grand National."

Tom's tortured expression evaporated when they all heard the sound of several motor cars stopping outside the house.

Mr. Carter stepped forward. "I suppose I should spare Bertram the task of opening his own door."

Even before anyone rang the bell, he opened the door and Evie and Tom saw the detective approaching, his attention fixed on a large notebook he carried.

CHAPTER 20

*D*etective Evans walked in. If he expressed surprise at finding Evie and Tom at Lynchfield Manor, Evie did not see it because she had her attention fixed on Mr. Carter to capture his reaction to the detective's arrival.

"You found it," Tom exclaimed.

"Yes, I believe so." The detective held up the journal, bound in red leather. "The constables have been scouring the immediate area. A short while ago, they spread out further and found an empty suitcase along with this. Since we don't know what the suitcase contained, we cannot say with any certainty what is missing. We only know the thief had no interest in a journal."

Had the suitcase's contents been more valuable than the silver and paintings Tom had seen stored in the motor car?

"I wonder if we can assume the suitcase contained

other valuable objects, smaller than the paintings and silver," Evie suggested.

The detective nodded. "It's quite possible."

"Whereabouts did you find it?" Evie asked.

"South of here. The constables are on their way to the village. Hopefully, someone will have seen something." As the detective spoke, he looked at Mr. Carter.

"Have you read the journal?" Mr. Carter asked.

"No, but I will."

"I must admit, I am intrigued by this mystery. While the thief did not care for the journal, the journal is quite possibly responsible for sending Julius to his death." Mr. Carter's eyes widened. "It's quite baffling."

Evie assumed the detective had reached the same conclusion she had. Mr. Carter did not seem to be perturbed by the appearance of the journal.

Nodding, the detective said, "If you'll excuse me, I need to speak with Lord Bertram."

"You'll find him in the library," Tom offered.

Evie felt torn between staying out of the detective's way and letting him do his job and following him inside the library to witness the new Lord Bertram's reaction to the news of the discovery.

In the end, she compromised, but only because the detective left the door to the library standing ajar.

Evie ambled toward the partially opened door and looked inside. Lord Bertram stood on a stepladder with a book in one hand and his other hand resting on a shelf, his fingers drumming an impatient tune.

The detective greeted him but Nigel Bowles, the new Lord Bertram, remained oblivious to his presence.

Finally, the detective caught his attention by raising his voice.

Lord Bertram swung around so quickly he teetered on the stepladder.

When the detective showed him the journal, Lord Bertram rejoiced.

"Thank heavens, you've found it. Although, I'm still not sure why you were looking for it."

He then asked if he'd like to stay for tea.

Evie turned and looked at Tom who stood a couple of paces away but had witnessed the entire scene.

"Does this clarify matters or does it deepen the mystery?" Mr. Carter asked.

"We're not exactly sure."

The detective emerged from the library, the journal still in his hand. At the same time, Alice Brown appeared, the tea tray wobbling slightly as she trudged toward the library. When she saw them standing out in the hall, the tray tipped slightly. Yelping, she managed to steady it.

"Alice? Is anything the matter?" Evie asked.

Giving a brisk shake of her head, Alice hurried into the library.

"Well, at least we get tea." Mr. Carter excused himself and followed Alice into the library.

The detective stood looking down at the journal. After a moment, he handed it to Evie. "Perhaps you can make some sense of this. I'll have a read through it later."

Doing her best to hide her surprise, Evie took it. She looked over her shoulder to make sure she wouldn't be overheard, and said, "We were thinking of driving into the village." She told him about wanting to speak with the auctioneer but also needing to return to the hunting lodge to contact Lotte Mannering. "I'm sure she has found something by now." Holding up the journal, she added, "I think we will all need to read this. Especially Henrietta. She knew Alexander Bertram and might be able to make sense of the information."

Looking pensive, the detective told them he wished to have another word with Alice. "I believe I am beginning to think like you, my lady. There was something about the way she reacted when she saw us."

"Us? I'm inclined to think she reacted to the journal."

"Yes, you are probably right."

As she and Tom left the manor house, Tom asked, "Has the detective earned any good points with that remark?"

"His professionalism remains above reproach." Evie lifted her chin. "The same cannot be said about his personal traits. Those are still in question."

She settled into the roadster and turned to the first page.

A short while later when they arrived at the village Evie looked up from the journal and sighed. "So far, I have read several entries about Alexander Bertram's journey to India. I shall never understand why people hunt for sport. It can't all be about the thrill of the chase." She shuddered and skimmed through the next page before putting the journal down. "He mentions a Mr. Carter. Do you think he is Roland Carter's father?"

"I couldn't tell you how old Roland Carter is," Tom said. "But he might be old enough to have been in his twenties back in 1901. Perhaps he traveled to India with Lord Bertram."

With the journal tucked under one arm and Holmes in the other, they focused on finding the auctioneer, trying their luck at the pub first.

When they asked about him, they were told, "He usually comes in for lunch."

Glancing at his watch, Tom signaled to a table. "We might as well sit here and do some more reading."

With Holmes happy to sit on her lap, Evie continued her reading, only skimming through some pages and skipping ahead. "He enjoyed going into great detail about shooting a tiger. Although, to his credit, the tiger had already attacked several villagers." She turned several pages and then stopped to read. "Oh, this is interesting. He mentions a Lady Hartfellows." Her eyebrows puckered.

Leaning in to read, Tom exclaimed, "One of eight children."

"Yes." She pointed to the next page. "She was twenty years his junior and he remarks on the number of children her sisters had already borne." Looking up, she drummed her fingers on the page. "I think he might have been considering marriage again."

Tom nodded. "Are you also thinking that put his life in danger?"

"If I say that, we will be putting a target on Lord Bertram."

"Which one?"

"Julius. He's the one who inherited Alexander's title."

"Well, he's dead, so I doubt he'll take exception to you pointing the finger at him."

"True. However, this could be a family killing spree and the new Lord Bertram could come under suspicion. Think about it. If Alexander Bertram had married a young woman who could bear him children, Julius would not have inherited the title."

Tom sat back. "You think Julius killed Alexander Bertram and now the new Lord Bertram killed Julius?"

Evie grinned. "That's as farfetched as I'm willing to be. For now, at least."

"If only Mr. Carter knew about your new theory. He'd be greatly relieved."

"Oh, he's guilty of something. I just haven't put my finger on it yet. But I will." Evie hummed under her breath.

"Are you making another connection?"

"No, I'm simply trying to make sense of something. When we arrived at the manor house and went to the library where we found the new Lord Bertram, he heard us coming in and turned. Yet, when the detective walked in carrying the journal, he called out his name but Lord Bertram didn't respond. Not until the detective raised his voice."

"What do you think that means?"

"I don't really know. Perhaps Lord Bertram caught sight of the journal and needed some time to think what he would say, how he would react."

The barkeep approached them and set down a bowl of water for Holmes. "That fellow you wanted to speak with has just arrived."

Thanking him, Tom and Evie looked toward the entrance and identified the man who had performed the auction.

He stood at the bar for a moment. When the barkeep approached him, they engaged in a conversation.

"Is he warning him about us?" Evie asked.

Tom shifted to the edge of his chair.

"What are you doing?"

"If the auctioneer heads for the door, I'll have to chase him."

Evie glanced at Tom. "Sometimes, I can't tell if you're being serious or not."

Tom adjusted his tie. "If he does head for the door, stay here, Countess. I'll take care of it."

"They are having rather a lengthy conversation," Evie noted.

"Now he's sizing you up."

"Me? I'm sure he's also looking at you."

"Not at all. I imagine he's just been told you're the

Countess of Woodridge and he is trying to decide how much money he can make out of selling your possessions."

The auctioneer approached them and introduced himself as Mr. Hutchins. Evie wasted no time in establishing her interest in acquiring certain information which he happily supplied because, as Tom had rightly surmised, he wished to make an impression and if she ever decided to put some of her possessions up for sale, could she please keep him in mind.

Mr. Hutchins confirmed her suspicions. The racehorse had been a last-minute inclusion in the auction. And, in his opinion, a reluctant one as Mr. and Mrs. Guildford had both looked and sounded quite angry about it.

Thanking Mr. Hutchins for the information, they excused themselves and left.

"Thank goodness he only wished to secure my business and didn't express any curiosity about our questions. I'm not ready to start broadcasting my activities to all and sundry."

"Are we going back to the hunting lodge? In your effort to extricate us from the auctioneer's clutches, you seem to have forgotten about lunch."

"I'm much too preoccupied to think about lunch. Although, Holmes might be getting hungry."

"You said that with a straight face."

Evie smiled at him. "Isn't that usually my line?"

"I see. You are trying your hand at teasing me." Tom opened the passenger door for her and added, "The hunting lodge it is. I'm sure you are eager to return there and share your findings with Henrietta and the others."

Evie thought about the rest of the information Mr. Hutchins had shared with them. "It must be done. We have no choice," she murmured. Why had Mr. Guildford said that?

Short of a confession, they would have no way of confirming if they had been forced to put the racehorse up for sale. She hoped the detective would have better luck. If, indeed, he wished to pursue that line of inquiry. She certainly couldn't justify her curiosity or tie it in with the murder case so he would have no reason to pursue it.

"It just occurred to me," Evie mused. "We have two mysteries in our hands."

"Three if you count the detective's veil of secrecy. Truth be known, I'm glad you haven't pressed for a confrontation."

"I've been too busy." Evie hugged Holmes against her. "By the way, thank you for getting me a puppy. He is adorable." Evie gazed into the distance. "Would you have looked for a puppy if we hadn't needed an excuse to call on Lord Bertram?"

"I doubt it." Tom glanced at her. "Are you about to make a point?"

She shrugged. "I'm trying to justify my interest in Mr. Carter. He might not have killed Lord Bertram but I insist he is somehow involved…"

"In what, exactly?"

"In… something." Evie rolled her shoulders.

"I can see this is making you tense."

"No, and that's something else Holmes is excelling at. He has a calming presence."

Driving up to the hunting lodge, they saw Edmonds walking around the Duesenberg and inspecting it for smudges. Mr. Miller stood near the corner of the lodge, his hands wrapped around the stick. A curtain shifted in the drawing room and Henrietta and Sara peered out. While upstairs, both Millicent and Caro stood by a window, looking down.

"We have a welcoming committee, Countess. Heaven only knows what awaits us inside."

Nodding, Evie said, "The only person I don't see is Toodles."

Tom tipped his hat down. "I know I have asked you this several times over the last few days… Do you have a plan?"

"Maybe we should get everyone a puppy. That would give them something else to focus on."

CHAPTER 21

The hunting lodge drawing room

$\mathcal{L}$eaving Tom to deal with Mr. Miller and Edmonds, Evie hugged Holmes close to her and went inside.

As she removed her coat, she thought she heard a scurry of footsteps coming from the rooms above as well as the drawing room.

Smiling, she pictured Caro and Millicent hurrying away from the window where they'd been standing keeping watch. She also imagined Henrietta and Sara rushing to settle down before she entered the drawing room.

"Right, here I go," she whispered.

To her surprise, Toodles had finally made an appearance and she sat by the fireplace. As expected,

Henrietta and Sara had moved away from the window and had sat with Toodles and were both engaged in lively conversation which Toodles seemed to be doing her best to ignore by keeping her focus on a book she was reading.

The moment they saw her, they acted surprised.

Henrietta pressed her hand to her throat. "We weren't expecting you back so soon. I'm afraid we have already had our luncheon. If we'd known you'd be returning early, we would have waited for you."

"Tom and I will be happy with some bread and cheese."

"I'm sure we can do better than that. We have been very nice to Edgar. He'll be happy to bring you something." Henrietta reached for the little bell near her and rang it.

"Grans. I see you found your way back. Have you been enjoying yourself?"

"I've been having a grand time with Mrs. Miller. Then these two sent out a search party for me. Now I'm sitting here and I've been listening to them rambling on."

Hurt by the remark, Henrietta was quick to say, "We have been trying to solve a mystery and we thought three heads would be better than two. Besides, you had been missing for quite some time and we were beginning to worry."

Setting Holmes down, Evie sat down and held the journal up. "This has turned up and I was rather hoping you would read it."

Henrietta's eyes brightened. "Is it Alexander's journal?"

"Alexander Bertram?" Toodles asked.

Surprised, they all turned to her.

'Mrs. Miller had a great deal to say about him. I mentioned Lord Bertram's death and that was enough to prompt her into talking about the family." Toodles moved her chair and sat next to Henrietta. "Hand it over."

Evie watched as they pored through it. For the first time that day she sat back and managed to empty her mind.

"Lady Hartfellows. The name rings a bell." Henrietta looked up from the journal. "Yes, now I remember. There was a rumor about him wanting to marry her."

Toodles chortled. "She had a lucky escape."

"Pardon?"

Evie couldn't tell if Henrietta looked surprised because Toodles had spoken or because of what she'd said.

"Let's just say he thoroughly enjoyed hunting and not just for game."

"He was a *Lothario*? That is news to me. I don't remember him paying particular attention to anyone. In fact, I'm surprised he even intended marrying again."

"You only ever came up here once a year." Toodles shrugged. "He was a busy man."

"Why are we hearing this now?"

"Because I only just told you about it."

Looking distraught, Henrietta asked, "Yes, but why didn't you mention it before?"

Toodles' eyes sparkled with mischief. "I had no reason to mention it."

"You might have said something while we were having lunch."

"The subject of Alexander Bertram didn't come up. You were both talking about Julius Bertram."

Huffing out a breath, Henrietta turned the page.

"You've missed a page," Sara said. "Oh, they appear to be stuck. It feels thicker than the other pages. I think there's something stuck between them."

Evie leaned forward to watch as Henrietta and Sara tried to separate the pages. When they succeeded, two photographs slipped out.

"Well, this is disappointing." Henrietta held one of the photographs up. "It's Alexander sitting at a table outside." She turned it. "1901. It only has a date. I assume he was in India. Most likely Assam."

"What makes you say so?" Evie asked.

"I knew he had a tea plantation and that's where the British East India Company set up."

Evie went to stand behind them so she could have a closer look. "He appears to be writing."

"Do you think he's writing on this journal?" Henrietta held the photograph up for a closer look.

He had a pen in one hand while the other hand rested on the table beside the journal, giving a clear indication of its size.

"This is a different one. It's much smaller," Henrietta said. "Heavens. That means we are still looking for a journal."

Sara picked up the other photograph. A group of men sat around a table enjoying a meal set up outside. They were all dressed in white suits. Holding the photograph up, Sara asked, "Do you recognize anyone?"

"Only Alexander." Henrietta pointed at his pocket. "That looks like the journal and it fits inside his pocket. Clearly, it's a different one."

When Tom walked into the drawing room he found them all huddled together.

"I wonder if one of those men was Mr. Carter's father." And, Evie thought, would Mr. Carter identify him if they showed him the photograph?

His presence there would almost put him at the scene of the accidental death.

"Surely Mr. Carter would have mentioned something about his father traveling with Alexander," Sara suggested.

"What are you all puzzling over?" Tom asked.

They all spoke at once with Henrietta waving the photograph.

"That's quite a find," Tom said.

"We think there might be another journal."

Before Evie could share her new suspicion, Tom said, "Perhaps that's what Mr. Carter was looking for in the attic."

Yes, but why would he want it?

Henrietta rubbed her eyes. "I might need stronger

spectacles or a magnifying glass. I can barely make out the details. I'm sure those platters of food look tantalizing."

Speaking of which...

Evie looked up. Where was Edgar?

"Tom, I'm afraid we have missed luncheon. I'm hoping Edgar will be able to bring us something." Evie glanced at the clock on the mantle. "Although, now that I think about it, the servants are probably having their luncheon."

Henrietta waved the photograph. "Can someone tell me if I'm imagining this? I think I see someone standing under the shade of a tree right here in the corner."

They took turns to look.

Toodles squinted. "If you can see that then there is nothing wrong with your eyes."

"So there is someone?"

"Most definitely."

Tom had a look and agreed. "Compared to the others in the photo, he looks much younger."

"I'm sure we have a magnifying glass somewhere." Evie considered asking Edgar to look for it but then she changed her mind. "I'll go look for it. I'm sure there is one in the study."

"I'll help you," Tom offered.

On the way out, Evie asked, "What did Mr. Miller have to say?"

Tom looked over his shoulder and lowered his

voice, "He's hoping Toodles will visit again. Apparently, she had a soothing effect on Mrs. Miller."

"I wouldn't be surprised if Toodles spends more time with the Millers. I believe she is still cross with Henrietta and Sara."

In the study, she rummaged through several drawers. "I hope the detective has some luck finding out who took the suitcase. At this point, I am in desperate need to solve at least one mystery."

"Have you heard from Lotte?"

"Oh, I'd forgotten about Lotte." She scooped in a breath. "No one mentioned anything so I assume she hasn't been in contact. Then again, she is busy with her own case." Humming under her breath, she added, "I'd hate to say it, but I would welcome a respite. My mind is spinning." Opening another drawer, she exclaimed, "Aha, I knew we had a magnifying glass."

Tom went to stand by the window. "The detective's arrived."

As Evie tidied up the desk, Tom said, "This looks interesting."

"What does?"

"Caro just rushed outside. If I'm correct in reading her body language, she means business."

"Perhaps you should give them some privacy," Evie said, her tone distracted. "Come away from the window."

"I think they're arguing. Caro's hands are fisted."

Evie surged to her feet and joined him by the window. "Good heavens. What is happening now?"

"I hate to say it, Countess, however, someone has to. I feel your letters failed to have the desired effect." Tom laughed. "Oh, this is getting serious. Caro is wagging her finger in his face. He is certainly getting a taste of what life will be like living with her."

"What is that supposed to mean?"

"It's the courtship game, Countess. Everyone is on their best behavior. It's only afterward, when it's too late, that you discover someone's true nature."

"Well, in case you are wondering, I have nothing to hide."

Tom laughed. "Yes, I'm well aware of what I'm getting into."

Glancing up at him, Evie gave him a bright smile. "I wonder if I can say the same about you? After all, you have been rather deceitful."

"Caro just stomped her foot."

"Oh, I missed it."

"Look, she's doing it again."

"Heavens." Evie swung away from the window. She knew she shouldn't interfere. She knew this had nothing to do with her.

"Countess? Where are you going?"

"I can't stand by and watch Caro being hurt."

Tom snorted. "I think Caro is the one doing the hurting."

Evie lifted her chin, squared her shoulders and marched outside. Halfway there, she told herself to remain calm. Then, stepping outside, she told herself to turn right around and go back inside.

Despite the sensible advice, she continued marching toward the couple.

As she neared them, the detective glanced up. Seeing Evie, he gave her a nervous smile. "Lady Woodridge."

Before Evie could think better of it, she blurted out, "Lord Evans."

CHAPTER 22

One mystery solved

"*S*he knows. *Her ladyship knows*," Caro wailed. Stomping her foot again, she swung away and rushed off toward the back of the hunting lodge.

"Caro," the detective called out. He gave chase but suddenly stopped and looked at Evie. "I can explain, my lady." Hesitating, he took a step toward her only to change his mind. Swinging away, he rushed after Caro.

Evie heard Tom approaching.

Her shoulders rose and fell. "Before you ask, I have no idea what just happened."

Tom sighed. "You did your best, Countess. That's all you can ever do."

"Mr. Winchester, your encouragement is beginning

to wear thin." Her best, so far, had earned her a throbbing headache.

"He's coming back," Tom murmured.

"Heavens. Could you please deal with him? I need to see how Caro is." She'd never seen her maid so upset. And what had she meant by her remark? "Oh. Oh, heavens. She knew about the detective's title and she thought I didn't know."

Tom snorted. "Would you have listened to me if I'd told you to stay out of their business?"

"Absolutely not. There's a reason why she's been keeping this from me and I'm willing to bet it has to do with Caro assuming I would take exception to the detective's title. Do you realize what this means?"

"Yes, Millicent is about to become your one and only lady's maid. At least one person will be happy."

"Tom, this isn't the time to tease me. Please make sure the detective is fit to carry on with his investigation." She had seen first-hand how disruptive emotional upheavals could be. Grumbling, Evie went inside in search of Caro. Along the way she encountered Edgar. She tried to hurry her step, but he caught her attention.

"My lady. I understand you wish to have a meal brought in."

"Not right this minute, Edgar."

"Very well, my lady." He hesitated and then cleared his throat. "There is something else… While I don't wish to burden you with minor concerns, there has been an incident in the kitchen."

Evie's hand rested on the balustrade. "And I trust you dealt with it in your usual efficient manner."

"Yes, absolutely, my lady." Edgar lifted his chin. "I slammed the door on the detective. I just thought you should know. I realize you might not approve of my actions." Edgar straightened. "However, at the time I felt the extreme steps needed to be taken because he upset Caro and I won't stand for that. I do hope I haven't overstepped."

"No, indeed, Edgar. You haven't." Evie took a step but Edgar had more to say.

"If he is to be barred from entering your house, my lady, I will need your permission to engage the footmen to assist me. You see, the detective tried to use force."

Evie sighed. "Tempers have flared, Edgar. I'm sure this will all be sorted out soon and in order to accomplish that the detective will need to come inside."

"Very well, my lady. But I will keep an eye on him."

"Bedlam," Evie whispered as she reached the landing. She turned to head toward the back of the lodge where the servants' rooms were located, only to hear the now familiar sound of bickering coming from her room.

She entered without hesitation and found Caro folding and unfolding a blouse. Millicent stood watching and nodding as Caro huffed and puffed.

"Millicent, would you give us a moment, please?"

"Milady." After a moment's hesitation, Millicent

found her voice. "With all due respect, Caro is very upset and she might need my support."

"Caro? Are you upset?"

Caro shrugged and nodded. "Millicent should stay, milady. Otherwise, she will hound me later on until I repeat everything you've said word for word."

"Very well." Evie eased the door closed and tried to settle her thoughts before speaking. However, for the briefest moment, Evie's thoughts strayed and fixed on the photograph of the men eating outdoors. What if they could identify the young man standing under the tree as Mr. Roland Carter? What would that mean to the investigation?

"I'm sorry you had to witness that altercation, milady. I promise it will never happen again."

She shook off the distraction and focused on Caro. "I take it you are cross with the detective."

Caro set the blouse down only to pick it up again. Giving a stiff nod, she resumed folding the blouse.

"May I ask what he did?"

Caro pressed her lips together. For a moment, it looked as if she wouldn't tell her. Then, her shoulders lowered. "He went behind my back when I explicitly told him not to."

"And what exactly did he do?"

"He went to see my parents," Caro wailed. "And... And he asked for my hand."

"Good heavens." Evie gave her a bright smile. "But isn't that wonderful news?"

Caro pressed her lips together and gave a vigorous shake of her head.

Millicent stepped forward. "Caro won't admit it, milady. She's afraid of what you will think and say when she becomes a lady."

Evie found herself lost for words. Millicent continued talking but Evie didn't hear her. Once again, her mind wandered to the photograph. She tried to dismiss the thought but it simply persisted.

This time, she wondered if the young man had been Julius Bertram. Had he been capable of killing his relative in order to gain the title and all that came with it?

Evie drew in a calming breath. "Caro, is this about the detective being a baron?"

"I'll be a lady, milady," Caro wailed.

"Heavens. Is that all that's worrying you?"

"It will make everything awkward between us and people will laugh at me and say I've risen above my station because I'm not really a lady and I won't know what to do or say."

"What nonsense," Millicent declared. "You've been a lady before. In fact, you've always enjoyed playing the role of Lady Carolina Thwaites, her ladyship's cousin thrice removed. Look, I'll even bob a curtsey. See. There's nothing to it."

Sighing, Evie sat on the edge of the bed. She would sort this business out first and then, she would deal with the rest.

An hour later...

"Countess?" Tom stood at the foot of the stairs, clearly waiting for her. "Has everything been sorted out?"

"Yes, you'll be pleased to know I don't have to shoot Lord Evans."

"That's good news. Does that mean he can come inside? He's been outside pacing up and down. I wouldn't be surprised if you find a trench out there."

"What did he have to say for himself?"

"He mumbled a great deal. From what I could put together, he wanted a career but he didn't want the title to stand in his way. However, the title does exist and there's no getting away from it."

"Is Evans the family name or the title?" Evie asked.

"There's a difference?"

"Yes, usually."

"I see. That makes sense. It's the title. He muttered a great deal about that saying he used the name Evans knowing he would one day inherit and he wanted to make the transition easy and avoid confusion. But now it's made matters worse and Caro doesn't want him because she's afraid of becoming a lady."

Evie raised her eyes heavenward. "I don't even want to imagine what Henrietta's reaction will be to all this. She seems to have forgotten about getting you a title and now..." Evie gave a determined nod. "I will deal with that later. Meanwhile, I suppose he should come in."

Tom wasted no time in inviting the detective inside.

The detective took a few tentative steps toward the house and stopped at the threshold. "My lady, I should apologize. If there has been any misunderstanding..." He glanced up. "Do you think Caro will agree to speak with me?"

"Perhaps." Evie's voice hitched and edged with impatience, "But right now, we are all waiting for news from you."

"Yes, of course. You'll be pleased to know we have found the thief." The detective looked up toward the stairs again and then at Evie, his forlorn expression replaced with a frown. Straightening, he said, "The constables had great success in chasing down the stolen goods from the suitcase. One of the store owners in the village remembered seeing a coster-monger they didn't recognize."

"A costermonger?"

"They travel around from village to village hawking goods. Anyhow, the constables drove around the area until they caught up with him. Lady Woodridge, you were right. The suitcase had been filled with small items. A collection of snuff boxes, silver frames and goblets were found in his possession."

"I see," Evie said and invited him to join her in the drawing room. "Well, that's one mystery solved."

"What's this?" Henrietta surged to her feet. "Does this mean we can now return to Halton House?"

"Henrietta, do sit down," Sara ordered. "The detective has only solved one mystery."

Looking mystified, Henrietta asked, "Which one?"

"The contents from the suitcase have been recovered, my lady."

Henrietta looked baffled. "And what does that mean?"

Sara leaned in and murmured an explanation.

"Oh, I see. We had assumed the killer had taken it but he didn't. Are we sure of that?"

"Yes, my lady. The costermonger was sighted several miles away when Lord Bertram was killed."

"In that case, we can put aside all thoughts about the suitcase and concentrate on this. Detective, we have discovered the existence of another journal, although I'm still not sure why we are so interested in it."

Sara leaned in and murmured an explanation which included mentioning Mr. Carter's name. When she finished, they both looked at Evie.

"Evangeline, when did you become so suspicious?"

When indeed.

Sara leaned in again and had another murmured conversation with Henrietta who exclaimed, "Oh, my apologies. Sara has just reminded me. I asked Julius Bertram about Alexander and he mentioned the journal and photograph. In a roundabout way, I suppose that means I am partially guilty…" Henrietta's eyes widened. "Oh, good heavens."

Remembering the magnifying glass she had found, Evie dug inside her pocket and retrieved it. "I hope this helps, Henrietta."

"Yes, and it might distract me from this feeling of guilt I'm suddenly experiencing."

As Henrietta studied the photograph, Evie walked to the fireplace and crouched down to give Holmes a scratch. Looking up, she told the detective about the photographs they had found.

"Well, we seem to be making progress," he said, although his tone sounded distracted.

Henrietta disagreed. "We now need to find this new journal. So far, we have ascertained Alexander Bertram's intention to marry. That puts Julius in a pickle. But he's dead so it doesn't really matter. However, it would help to know if he had something to do with Alexander's death."

"That reminds me." Evie straightened. "I need to contact Lotte Mannering. I asked her to hunt down some information that might have been printed in 1901 about Lord Bertram's death."

Evie left them to discuss the photograph and made her way to the study. The fact Lotte hadn't contacted her probably meant she hadn't found anything or, indeed, she hadn't had the time to devote to the search.

To her annoyance, Evie's telephone call couldn't be put through.

Tom walked in and found her grumbling under her breath. "Trouble in paradise?"

Evie looked up. "Have you ever noticed how a deer reacts to danger?"

Tom nodded. "They become alert, suddenly stiffen and if the danger is real it can jump into action and run for its life."

"And then? When the danger is over…"

Tom thought about it for a moment. "It goes back to being relaxed."

"Yes."

"And your point is?"

"I'm still waiting for that moment when I can sit back, relax and think about nothing."

Tom laughed. "I would give you five minutes and then you'd start fidgeting."

"Are you suggesting I thrive while in a constant state of alertness?" Instead of waiting for his answer, Evie jumped to her feet. "Let's go for a walk."

"And there's your answer."

Tom helped her into her coat and as they walked out, said, "I think you're forgetting someone."

"Not this time. Holmes looked quite happy curled up by the fireplace. Come on, the Miller's cottage is not far from here. If we're lucky, we might get a cup of tea."

Evie slipped her hands inside her pockets and wondered if she should get a stick. Something long to poke things with. "I think you're right. I'm about to start fidgeting."

"And then, are you going to start bickering?"

Not quite understanding the remark, Evie frowned. Then, she made the connection. "Yes. You're right. I have developed an addiction for action and if I am denied, I might well start bickering."

When they reached the edge of the clearing, they followed a well-trodden path. At one time, Evie had been able to identify every tree and wild flower growing in the area. Now, her mind remained fixated on their puzzle.

"We mustn't be sidetracked by Alexander's death in India but a part of me feels that discovering the truth could be crucial to finding out if Julius killed himself or if he was killed." There had to be some sort of connection, Evie insisted.

"At least you are no longer fixating about Mr. Carter."

"Who says I'm not?"

"I suppose it would also help to identify the young man standing under the tree."

"Absolutely and I can think of three possible answers. It's either Mr. Carter, Julius Bertram or someone we haven't met and who doesn't play a role in the mystery. Which, of course, would mean we are barking up the wrong tree."

"Countess, there's no such thing as a false trail." Tom laughed at Evie's look of surprise. "Since my last words of encouragement failed to impress you, I thought I'd try to come up with something different."

"That's very thoughtful of you, Tom."

The aroma of bread caught their attention first and then they saw the cottage. A neat garden surrounded the stone building with a vegetable garden to the side and beyond that a stable.

"I do hope we won't be intruding."

Tom grinned. "I hope we are. In fact, I hope they are right in the middle of a feast and urge us to join them. Remember, we haven't had lunch yet."

A hard thud had them both stopping dead in their tracks.

Evie cringed. "I am developing an intense dislike for that sound."

Tom pointed ahead. "It's Mr. Miller. He's chopping wood."

When he saw them, he tipped his hat back and nodded.

"I'm rather fond of his economical gestures," Evie mused and, raising her voice, said, "Mr. Miller, I do hope we haven't caught you at an inopportune moment."

"Yes," Tom agreed. "We feared you might have been having lunch."

Mr. Miller looked toward the cottage. "Mrs. Miller and I were just about to sit down. I can always tell by the aroma of bread."

"In that case, we won't keep you." Evie thought she heard Tom whimper. "Was that you?" she whispered.

"Yes. I won't deny it."

"Since you've come all this way, my lady, would you like to come in for a cup of tea. Mrs. Miller will surely insist."

"Oh, yes. That would be lovely." Turning to Tom, she murmured, "I could definitely do with a change of subject."

They followed the caretaker inside and greeted his wife. Her light blue eyes were enhanced by a mop of red hair gathered into a neat bun. She wore a floral printed blouse with the sleeves rolled up to her elbows.

"My lady, if I'd known you were coming I would have prepared something. As it is, I only have a stew."

"That sounds delicious," Tom said.

Evie felt compelled to say, "Oh, we couldn't possibly impose."

Mr. Miller shook his head. "Mrs. Miller will insist, won't you, Mrs. Miller?"

Evie eyed a broomstick in the corner near the hearth and wondered if Mrs. Miller would be chasing her husband around the house with it when they left, complaining that he hadn't warned her of their arrival.

"It's settled," Mrs. Miller declared. "It will be a hearty meal but nothing compared to what you are used to up at the big house and I do apologize for that."

Evie assured her she had grown up eating her fair share of stews prepared by their Irish cook and quite looked forward to it.

They spent the next half hour talking about the hunting in the area and an upcoming fair which Mrs. Miller was preparing for as she always entered something. Especially now with so many good cooks no longer around because they'd either succumbed to the Spanish flu or had moved away.

"Too many losses," Mrs. Miller bemoaned. "Not to mention all those young men not returning from the war. There is still resentment for those who didn't fight." The kettle boiled and Mrs. Miller jumped to her feet and prepared some tea.

The conversation changed to Evie's idea of opening

up the lodge, something Mr. Miller said he would definitely enjoy.

Thanking Mrs. Miller for her hospitality, Evie decided she'd succeeded in clearing her head and they should return to the hunting lodge.

As they made their way out, she turned to Mr. Miller. "What did Mrs. Miller mean when she spoke about lingering resentment?"

Mr. Miller dismissed the remark. "Rumors abound in small villages. Mrs. Miller can sometimes get carried away. Especially when she's worried about something and she would have been worried about you not liking the stew."

Evie assured him, "I will make a point of sending her a thank you note. And it would be lovely if she could share her secret with my cook. Please ask her for me."

"That will definitely put a bounce to her step, my lady. Thank you."

Enjoying the feeling of contentment experienced after a hearty meal, they made their way back to the lodge.

"This visit to the Miller's cottage did you a world of good, Countess."

"Yes, they are a lovely couple," Evie said distractedly and resumed thinking about the rumor. Clearly, Mr. Miller didn't think there was much substance to the claim.

"And yet," Evie murmured, "I have no trouble making a connection."

CHAPTER 23

The hunting lodge

"That is the wildest theory you have come up with to date," Tom said after Evie finished sharing her thoughts with him.

Evie had a hard time convincing Tom of her new suspicion, but it made perfect sense to her.

She had threatened Mrs. Guildford with the possibility of being questioned by the police. Now she needed to make good on her threat. Surely, Mrs. Guildford would reveal all to the detective.

The couple had two sons. They hadn't served. The lingering resentment Mrs. Miller had mentioned had suggested there had been some men who had deliberately avoided going to war.

With the right connections, Evie thought, it would be possible to pull strings and arrange to be excluded.

Earlier, she had wondered what the Guildfords could have been threatened with. Knowledge of such an arrangement could certainly be used against them. Especially so soon after the war.

"I remember Alice Brown telling us Mr. and Mrs. Guildford's sons had gone to America soon after war broke out. I didn't think to question it at the time but surely it raises a few questions. How did they avoid serving?"

"Perhaps they were not fit to serve," Tom suggested.

"How convenient that they should both be excluded. Actually, how is someone excluded?"

"Physical ailment is all I can think of." Tom shrugged. "I'm sure there are plenty of reasons. I'm afraid I have to say it, Countess. I suspect you are grasping at straws."

"Am I? We shall soon see. The detective has solved the mystery of the missing suitcase, now I'd like to solve this niggling mystery before it drives me batty."

Tom grinned. "Don't take it the wrong way, Countess, but I think your relatives have already done that."

When they arrived at the lodge, they were met by the detective in the hall. Evie had a hard time convincing him he should question Mrs. Guildford. "I told Mrs. Guildford it was essential to establish some facts in order to arrive at a motive. Detective, if you use your authority, I'm sure she will open up to you and reveal the truth."

The detective looked puzzled.

Out of the corner of her eye, she saw Holmes sitting by the door to the drawing room. Evie crouched down and he came trotting toward her. Picking him up, she straightened.

"This harks back to my earlier suspicion about Mr. Carter," Evie persevered.

Tom nodded. "Apparently, he looked quite evil when he won the bid. Personally, I think it might have been a look of supreme satisfaction and triumph. I'm sure I would have looked the same if I had been allowed to bid on the racehorse."

"This is the racehorse that placed at the Grand National?" the detective asked.

Trying to get everyone back on track, Evie said, "No stone left unturned, detective." She searched for her gloves. Remembering the detective had earlier stayed behind at Lynchfield Manor to have a word with Alice Brown, she asked, "By the way, did your conversation with Alice Brown yield any results?"

"Not really. She explained her reaction by saying she heard a thud and she panicked because it reminded her of the sound she heard when Lord Bertram fell to his death. She managed to talk herself out of it. However, when she made her way to the library, she found us in the hall. For a moment, she thought something had happened to the new Lord Bertram and that's why she reacted the way she did."

"Do you believe her?"

"It sounds like a reasonable explanation."

"I'm not convinced." Evie shook her head. "However, we can talk about that later. Meanwhile, we should set out now. Who knows if Mr. and Mrs. Guildford are still at the house."

The detective didn't move. "Lady Woodridge. As much as I appreciate your input, I'm afraid I can't justify questioning Mrs. Guildford. Yes, there might be some sort of connection, but I really fail to see what it might be. I can't make a case out of nothing."

"Are you telling me you won't do it?" Evie could not have sounded more frustrated or disappointed.

"I'm afraid it is simply too far-fetched."

Evie gave a stiff nod and marched out of the lodge.

Shrugging, Tom followed her. "Countess, are you going off in a huff?"

"Indeed, I am."

"Will I be driving you somewhere?"

"Yes, please."

When they settled in the roadster, Tom looked at her but remained silent.

"I suppose you wish to know where we are going."

"If you like, we could sit here until you feel better," Tom suggested.

"I will only feel better once I know we have done everything in our power to catch the culprit. When Lotte Mannering hears of my failure, I wouldn't be surprised if she decides to dissolve our partnership."

"Now, now, Countess. You really mustn't be so hard on yourself. You know Lotte would be the first person to say you can't solve every case."

Despite not knowing where they were going, Tom drove off, albeit at a sedate pace.

After they had put a reasonable distance between themselves and the hunting lodge, he said, "I must say, you are to be commended for not using blackmail on the detective."

"I'm not sure I know what you mean."

"You could have twisted his arm by letting him know how much influence you have on Caro. Luckily for him you are not that type of person."

"Manipulative?" Evie laughed. "You seem to forget I manipulated everyone into coming here. But you're right, I suppose I shouldn't be so hard on myself. As for Caro, I would never stand in the way of her happiness." After a moment, Evie laughed. "It is an interesting turn of events."

"Yes, and your household is becoming quite colorful."

When they reached the village, Tom slowed down. "To the left is the Guildford house. You could ignore that suspicion and move on to something else. If we turn right, we can go to Lynchfield Manor and you can work your magic on Lord Bertram."

"For some strange reason, Holmes wagged his tail when you mentioned going to Lynchfield Manor."

"Are we now following Holmes' tail?"

"It's the only sign we have."

Tom glanced down at Holmes. "Are you sure, buddy?"

"Just in case you didn't see it, his tail wagged again."

"I suppose it makes no difference where we go. In the mood you are in, someone will be compelled to tell all."

Instead of turning toward the road leading to the Guildford house, Tom headed in the opposite direction. It seemed he had decided to distract her with a pleasant drive in the country.

She didn't blame him. At some point, they would need to abandon their hunt for the truth.

Despite the distraction provided by the scenic landscape, every thought Evie entertained brought her back to thinking about what someone or other had said or done.

Evie knew she had relied on observation. How people reacted could say a great deal about how they felt or what they were thinking or even if they were hiding something.

Lord Bertram had died at his home and there had been less than a handful of people present. Nigel Bowles, Mr. Carter, Alice Brown and the other housemaid. They had also entertained the possibility of someone else. A mysterious fifth person...

In any case, it should have been easy to establish people's guilt or innocence but in order to do that, they needed physical proof and motive.

They had scrutinized everything everyone had said and Evie had even employed her imagination to delve and poke further, something she had no trouble doing as everyone had behaved in an odd or questionable manner.

Tom slowed down and finally brought the roadster to a stop. To her surprise, they were outside the gates to Lynchfield Manor. In fact, from where they sat, they could see the house.

"You took the long way around."

Tom looked at his watch. "I drove around for a full hour. You must have been lost in your thoughts."

"Anyone would think you want to give me closure."

"Would that be such a bad thing?"

"I suppose you are right. We don't have to solve every case." She sat back and studied the house. "You'd never guess someone had died in that house," Evie mused. "It looks untouched by tragedy. It's only through our perception that we look at it and know something happened there."

She had employed all her limited abilities. Now, they could turn around, drive away and never think about it again.

"Opportunity and timing," she murmured. "A costermonger comes along, pokes around the place. He enters the stables and sees a motor car and the items stored in it and he decides to steal the most convenient one. A suitcase. Then, there was our own timing. We arrived at the house moments before Lord Bertram jumped to his death."

"Don't forget the detective. If you hadn't sent him a letter requesting his presence, he would not have driven out this way. Indeed, he would not have seen us drive through the village. I think we should consider ourselves lucky that he did. I can't imagine how you would have fared with another detective on the case."

Had someone in that house taken advantage of an opportunity? Had they seen Lord Bertram in a state of panic? Had they chased him to his death?

Evie sighed. "Thank you for the drive. I believe I am now ready to accept my failure. Oh, well, I suppose we should head back. If we're lucky, this trip will have settled everyone's jittery behavior and now we can all return to some sort of normality."

"Of course," Tom said, "there is also the wedding to plan."

"Heavens. Yes. And Henrietta will no doubt resume her efforts to find you a title." Evie sighed. "We might even find ourselves back in square one."

Tom changed gears and maneuvered the motor to make the turn. However, he saw a motor car heading their way so he had to wait.

Instead of driving on, the motor car slowed down.

Evie leaned forward. "Is that the detective's motor car?"

Tom tipped his hat back. "I believe it is."

The motor came to a stop. The detective climbed and approached them.

"Detective?"

"Yes, my lady, I changed my mind. Actually, my mind was changed for me. Caro gave me an earful for not listening to you."

"And?"

"I have just come from having an official conversation with Mr. and Mrs. Guildford."

Tom looked at Evie. "By any chance, is Holmes' tail wagging?"

"Yes, it is."

The detective looked toward the house. "Your instincts about Mr. and Mrs. Guildford hiding something were quite correct. One of the reasons they decided to sell their property and move away is because they knew the truth would all eventually come out. It seems the gossip in the village hasn't died down and people still question how some men managed to avoid serving in the war. Specifically, their two sons who are now living in America."

"They pulled strings," Evie said.

"Yes."

"What about Mr. Carter? My entire theory was based on him using some sort of information to coerce them into putting the horse up for sale."

The detective gave a pensive nod. "I must admit, I am astonished by the connection you made. More so as you ended up attending the auction out of sheer curiosity and chance."

"Detective, you have us both on edge. What else did you discover?"

"During Mr. Carter's numerous visits to Lord Bertram, he became acquainted with the rumors flying around the village and decided to look into it. He discovered Mr. Guildford had worked at the War Department. While he resigned his post just before the war, he still had connections and quite a lot of influence."

Evie gasped.

"It seems Mr. Carter has a knack for digging up information. Anyhow, when he learned what Mr. and Mrs. Guildford had managed to do, he realized they might not want the news to get out."

"And so," Evie said, "he used the information to his advantage."

Tom nodded. "As leverage to force them to put the racehorse up for sale."

"Precisely." The detective nodded. "He wanted to make it look as legitimate as possible."

"Well, detective. It seems you have solved another mystery."

"You are much too modest, my lady." Once again, he looked toward the house. "This isn't something I can charge Mr. Carter with. Indeed, it's Mr. Guildford who should be investigated. However, knowing what Mr. Carter did does raise a few questions. If he is the type of man to use knowledge to his advantage, did he have something he could use against Lord Bertram?"

"I suspect he must know a great deal about the Bertram family," Evie offered. "Both from his and his father's association with them."

"Well, I think I might just go and have a chat with him. Feel free to join me."

Evie and Tom both jumped at the opportunity.

"By the way," the detective said. "Lady Henrietta made use of your magnifying glass and noticed something significant. The young man standing under the tree has his thumb hitched on the pocket of his coat."

"What does that mean?" Evie asked.

"The pocket is sagging. She remembered Julius Bertram had the habit of hitching his thumb on the pocket."

Evie gasped and nodded. "I remember Julius Bertram greeting me. He had his thumb hitched on his pocket."

Heavens, Julius Bertram had been in India during that fateful last journey.

CHAPTER 24

The truth will out

*A*s they walked up to the house, Evie remembered Julius Bertram's greeting the first time they'd visited.

It's the pigs you see...

She had met her share of eccentric characters. Some were even related to her. While she had been ready to witness some sort of odd behavior, under different circumstances, she might have found Lord Bertram quite amusing.

That thought led her to wonder what might have been if she hadn't poked her nose into his business.

Evie shuddered. Had she been responsible for triggering the events that had unfolded after their visit?

If she shared her thoughts with Tom, she knew he

would provide sage and practical advice that would steer her away from the burden of guilt she sensed building up.

Identifying him as the young man standing under the tree should have provided them with some clarity. Instead, they had more questions. Even the detective had no idea what to do with the information.

Scooping in a breath, Evie turned her thoughts to the pigs. She realized a swift change of subject always worked wonders. Her shoulders eased down and she smiled.

The new Lord Bertram would take care of the pigs. He had already shown a keen interest in them by searching for appropriate books to read on the subject.

Heavens, that brought her full circle. Once again, she thought about Julius Bertram and his pigs and his obvious preoccupation with them.

Evie's step faltered. "Detective, when you searched the house for the journal, did you have a look around the pig pen?"

"The pig pen?" he repeated.

"Yes, Lord Bertram had a great fondness for his pigs. He looked after them himself."

"Is this another one of your intuitive suspicions, my lady?"

"No stone left unturned, detective." While she and Tom had been ready to abandon their investigation, Evie knew that if they had driven back to the hunting lodge, they could have taken some time to clear their heads and, perhaps, something else might have occurred to them. Given enough time, she felt sure they would fit all the pieces together and solve the puzzle.

"We are already here, detective. It certainly won't hurt to have a look. Mr. Carter's comeuppance can wait."

They walked around the house and headed to the stables. Beyond them, another smaller building housed the pigs.

As they made no effort to conceal their intentions, they expected someone from the house to come out and question their presence, but no one did.

Pushing the gate open, they walked in and were greeted by snorts and grunts.

"Nice pigs," Evie remarked.

"Wessex Saddlebacks," the detective said. "They have the distinct black body with white band around the trunk."

"You know about pigs, detective?"

He gave a distracted shrug. "I've attended enough country fairs to have picked up some basic information."

Apart from a toolshed at the back of the building which contained every tool imaginable, they found nothing that could be of interest in the case.

Evie's shoulders slumped. "There's nothing here. Perhaps we should go inside and have that chat with Mr. Carter. At the very least, we can make him feel dreadfully uncomfortable. He ought to be ashamed of his underhanded behavior."

Tom stepped forward, picked up a hay fork and began prodding around. "Countess, your instincts always produce something of interest. You were suspicious about Mr. Carter and he turned out to be a scoundrel."

Being methodical, Tom worked from one end to the other plunging the fork into the stacks of hay. Finally, near the end of his thorough search and just as they'd been about to give up hope, he exclaimed, "Here's something."

Evie and the detective rushed forward and watched as Tom used the hay fork to dislodge the hay and reveal a wooden chest.

They didn't waste time celebrating their find. When the contents were revealed they plunged right in, everyone reaching for one of the many journals stacked inside the chest.

"This one is dated 1897." Evie turned to the last page. "And it ends at the start of 1898."

The detective had picked one up for the following year.

"I have one for 1900. Are we reading them or are we just looking at the dates?" Tom asked.

"I think we are looking for the last one Alexander Bertram wrote. That would be in 1901. It will be smaller than these ones."

After a meticulous search, they all looked around as if seeking another lead.

The detective tipped his hat back. "It's not here."

Tom turned to Evie. "Countess, you need to work your magic and come up with another hunch."

"It's obvious. Someone took it."

"And?" Tom encouraged her.

Evie shrugged. She pictured Henrietta declaring this had to mean something. Indeed, it had to be the key to solving the puzzle.

"Come on, Countess. Engage your imagination and weave a tale."

"Is that what you think I do?"

"Isn't it?"

"I prefer to think of it as observing and then interpreting what I see." Evie huffed. "But I'll do my best. Let's see. 1901. Since finding the other journal, this has become the key journal we have been curious about. That's the year Alexander Bertram died. We know he kept two journals. The one the detective found and the one we saw in the photograph which fitted inside his pocket."

Tom nodded. "The one he clearly took to India."

Evie shook her head. "He took both journals with him. Remember, I told you about the tiger he hunted. This other one must be a more personal journal."

The detective swung away and paced around. "We are missing something obvious. So far, we've been looking for a journal that might provide information. The sort of information that can turn into a motive for killing someone. Until now I hadn't suspected Mr. Carter, however, Lady Woodridge's observations made it possible to discover a wrongdoing." The detective turned to face her. "I don't recall you being obsessively suspicious of the new Lord Bertram."

"No, although he did act somewhat suspiciously when you showed him the journal you had recovered from the suitcase." Looking down at the ground, Evie shook her head. "At this point, we would have to rely on someone, or rather, the culprit, doing or saying something to give themselves away."

"In other words," Tom said, "there is no such thing as a perfect crime because the truth will out."

Evie looked at Tom. "There is one other person we haven't considered."

Tom and the detective gave her their full attention.

"June, the housemaid." When they didn't respond, Evie shrugged. "That, gentlemen, is my wildest idea to date. We know Alice Brown was in the kitchen since that's where the screams came from and June said she'd been upstairs dusting."

"Why would she kill Lord Bertram?" the detective asked. Seeing Tom and Evie's blank expressions, he smiled and explained, "I'm afraid I still need to consider motive as a driving force."

Evie wanted to suggest they return to the hunting lodge and discuss it with the others.

"How old do you think she is?" Tom asked.

Cringing, Evie said, "I've never been any good at guessing a person's age."

"Somewhere in her twenties," the detective suggested. "Too young to have been around in 1901."

They all fell silent again.

Evie kicked the ground with the tip of her shoe while Holmes wagged his tail and nuzzled her chin.

Lifting her gaze by tiny increments, Evie said, "Too young to have been around in 1901. What if she was *born* in 1901?"

Tom studied her for a moment before saying, "Toodles suggested Alexander Bertram had been a *Lothario*." Seeing the detective's puzzled expression, Tom added, "She learned this from Mrs. Miller, the caretaker's wife."

"Are you suggesting June could be related to Alexander Bertram?" the detective asked. "A by-blow?"

"Detective, I'm being creative and I'm afraid this is all I can come up with." Evie managed a smile. "I wonder if that's the sort of information Alexander Bertram might have written down in his journal?"

Tom crossed his arms and frowned. "Something doesn't make sense. We assume Julius Bertram put the journal in the suitcase, possibly because it contained vital information and he kept the other journals in the chest. What about the one that is missing?"

"Perhaps he destroyed it because it contained something truly significant," Evie suggested.

Tom didn't agree. "He kept the journal with the photograph which put him at the scene of Alexander Bertram's death. That's quite significant. I'm afraid this might be a case of him taking the secret to his grave. We will never know what he intended doing with it. Then again, according to Alice Brown, he hadn't really been himself. Perhaps he misplaced it." Tom's eyes brightened. "Maybe, what we witnessed in the library was Julius rummaging through his books looking for the missing journal."

Evie let her mind wander back to June. Why hadn't they suspected the housemaid? Admittedly, her theory sounded outrageous.

She pictured June stumbling upon the journals and reading through them until she found something that affected her personally. Perhaps even proof of her paternity.

Liking the idea, she nodded. "It is possible."

"What is?" Tom asked.

"June might have found the journals. She works here and she could have seen Julius Bertram in the pig pen going through the trunk."

Tom smiled at her. "Countess, you always start with a wild idea. Then, you embellish it and suddenly, it all becomes feasible."

"I'll take that as a compliment." Evie gave him a bright smile and went on to suggest, "We could ask Alice Brown about June. She might know something about her background. If we are going to pursue this, detective, we should tread with care. If there is any substance to my theory about June's paternity, I doubt June would wish for this information to become public. Illegitimacy still carries a stigma."

Once again, they fell silent with only the sound of the snorting pigs disturbing their thoughts.

Evie hugged Holmes against her and strolled around. What sort of information could June have stumbled upon? What if it had been something significant enough to prompt her to take action against Julius Bertram?

"I think I might need to have a chat with the housemaid. However, as you suggested, I'll make discreet inquiries and approach Alice Brown first."

Evie glanced at the detective. He hadn't sounded enthusiastic and she didn't blame him.

June's age and possible paternity were the only reasons to suspect her as they would justify her involvement. If they were on the right track and June had discovered Alexander Bertram had fathered her...

"Oh, heavens. I'm afraid my imagination is now running away with me. Now I'm thinking about the young man standing under the tree in the photograph."

"Countess, are you about to suggest Julius killed Alexander?"

"As you said earlier, I think I'm clutching at straws. I'm not entirely comfortable with suspecting the housemaid. We already know Mr. Carter enjoys availing himself of information and using it for his own benefit. I'm more inclined to think he found the journal and used the information in it to..." Evie floundered. His relationship with Lord Bertram had been quite friendly. Had he been capable of blackmailing him?

"I've said this before, but it really would help to know how Lord Bertram fell to his death," Tom mused and looked at the detective.

"I'm afraid the findings remain inconclusive."

Evie suspected Tom felt as uncomfortable as the detective about her latest theory. She didn't blame him. The moment the detective led up to the suggestion she had been born out of wedlock, June would be distressed beyond comprehension. Evie certainly couldn't imagine what her own reaction would be.

Tom gave a determined nod. "We found one journal, if we put our minds to it, we can find the other one. Once we know what it contains, we can proceed with more confidence."

As if by agreement, they all exited the pig pen. Seeing the sun hanging low over the roof, Evie looked at her watch and cringed.

"I would prefer it if we headed back to the lodge." In other words, she thought, the detective could take care of the unpleasant task of accusing the housemaid.

Tom cupped her elbow. "Very well. For what it's worth, I think you are being incredibly sensible. Besides, Holmes looks like he's pining for a cozy place by the fire."

"Yes, he does look rather forlorn. Do you think he might need another puppy for company?"

Tom laughed just as a door closed and determined footsteps sounded along the gravel path surrounding the house.

"Is that the housemaid?" Tom asked. He shielded his eyes for a better look. "It is."

At that precise moment, June looked up and saw them. Her step faltered. Then, clutching the bag she carried against her chest, she put her head down and hurried off.

"I really should speak with her now," the detective said and walked toward her.

The detective called out her name. The housemaid looked over her shoulder and instead of stopping, she hurried her step and disappeared around the corner.

"Either he startled her or she doesn't want to talk to the detective," Tom said.

"Either way, it's a bad move on her part. Why try to flee when he will most likely catch up with her?"

"Because she's guilty of something?" Tom suggested.

Alice Brown appeared at the back door and looked toward them. Acknowledging her, Evie and Tom walked up to her.

"Alice," Evie greeted her.

"What's happened? I thought I saw someone run by." The young woman's cheeks flushed a deep shade of crimson.

Evie remembered her reaction when she'd seen them in the hall. "Alice, is there something you wish to share with us?"

The detective appeared from around the corner, his hand wrapped around June's arm. While his other hand held what appeared to be a small book.

Alice Brown gasped and pressed her hands to her cheeks.

"I think we're about to have some of our questions answered."

CHAPTER 25

"*W*hat happened?" Alice Brown asked as the detective moved past her and walked into the house.

He looked over his shoulder and said, "If I could please have a moment alone with June."

Evie felt almost grateful he hadn't invited them to sit in on the interview. She turned to Alice. "I'm afraid June might be in trouble."

"What sort of trouble?"

Evie tilted her head. "I suspect you know, Alice."

The housemaid took a deep swallow.

"Did you see her take the journal? Is that why you reacted the way you did when you saw the detective holding a journal?"

Alice shook her head.

"Alice. If you know something, you really should tell us."

Her shoulders sagged. Lowering her head, she said,

"I told her she would get into trouble, but she wouldn't listen. A couple of days ago I saw her slip it into her bag. She said it might as well belong to her because it was the only proof she had. I have no idea what she meant by that and I didn't ask because she pushed me out of the way and rushed out of the house."

Proof of what?

"Countess, I suspect you might have been right to suggest what you did."

"You say you saw her with it a couple of days ago. Was that before or after Lord Bertram's death?"

"Just after. In fact, it was after everyone left."

June had kept it even after Julius' death. What had she planned on doing with it?

Alice looked toward the kitchen door. "She shouldn't be alone. June gets upset easily."

"This definitely won't bode well for June," Tom murmured.

"I'm trying to avoid forming opinions until we get the full picture." Alice had said June kept looking over shoulder expecting to see Julius' ghost. Did she have it in her to push someone off a roof?

After half an hour, the detective emerged from the house, the journal in his hand.

He looked at Alice. "I think June could do with a cup of tea."

Evie's eyebrows shot up.

When Alice Brown disappeared inside, the detective gestured toward the front of the house.

"I've spoken with the new Lord Bertram and he has

agreed. Under the circumstances, no charges can be pressed." He waved the journal. "There is enough in here to convict Julius Bertram of killing Alexander. Of course, they are both dead. As there is no point in pursuing this, and Lord Bertram wouldn't want any of it to become public knowledge, he feels it would be best for everyone concerned to let it all go."

Despite her eagerness to learn more, Evie asked, "What about June?"

The detective handed her the journal. "June does feel responsible for Julius' death. As she said, she had been dusting. But not at the time of his death. She had found the journal in his bedroom floor earlier that day and had assumed it had fallen out of his pocket. Considering what it contains, heaven only knows why he didn't destroy it."

Evie's eyebrows curved up. "Are you going to tell us or will I have to read it for myself?'

"Turn to the dogeared page."

Evie found the page and read it. "Julius not pleased with my intention to marry Lady Hartfellows. Less so with my desire to settle money on the child. I will take care of it. As well as Mariah Rogers. Of course, marriage is out of the question but my child will have all the advantages I can provide him or her with. The child will be born in June." Evie looked up. "Alexander *was* June's father?"

"I am quite astonished myself," the detective remarked. "You turned your attention to the one person we hadn't suspected and then you played around with dates." He shook his head. "How you managed it, I have no idea. Anyhow, determined to get to the truth, June decided to confront Julius. Of course, she already had proof since Alexander had named her mother, Mariah Rogers. She encountered him just as he was coming out of the library. When he saw her holding the journal, she says he became distraught."

"And he headed for the front door?" Evie asked.

"Yes, indeed. He must have realized June's discovery meant it was all over. He would be charged with murder. If you read further, you'll find specific references to Alexander's concerns and Julius' threats."

"And so he decided to take his own life?" Tom asked.

The detective nodded. "We really can't know for sure. However, he rushed past her and fled up the stairs. She chased after him, but she was too late. When she heard Alice's scream, she found herself in the corridor. Panicking, she hid in one of the rooms." He gestured to the journal. "As I said, there is more. Alexander Bertram worried about Julius' reaction to the news of his impending marriage. You see, he became quite aggressive and threatened him. Fearing for his life, Alexander sent him away. There is a brief mention of an incident. He only says he came close to being hit by a misfired shot. Clearly, the next shot got him."

"That doesn't necessarily mean Julius went ahead and killed him."

The detective shrugged. "Should we take the word

of a housemaid who was deprived of an inheritance or believe in the innocence of a man who obviously kept this information from her?"

Evie skimmed through several pages. "Did June explain why she kept this hidden from you?"

The detective slipped his hands inside his pockets. "She said it was all the proof she had. Her mother had always refused to say her father's name. But she did organize for June to come and work at the house. For all we know, she might have wanted to eventually reveal the truth to her daughter."

He looked toward the house. "Lord Bertram will have a lot of soul searching to do. I hope he makes good on Alexander Bertram's plans to provide for his child."

"He will," Evie said with certainty and waved the journal. "After all. This is not the sort of information he would want made public." Smiling at Tom, she added, "You see, Mr. Winchester, I'm not above blackmail."

EPILOGUE

The hunting lodge

*B*ack at the hunting lodge, Evie, Tom and the detective took turns to share the news with everyone.

Once they overcame the shock of hearing about Julius Bertram's actions all those years ago, they turned their attention to the rest.

"So, Mr. and Mrs. Guildford are guilty of keeping their sons out of the war. What will happen to them?" Henrietta asked.

"I don't really know if their actions carry any penalties, Henrietta. It has been two years since the war ended. However, feelings are still raw and I suspect they might be sanctioned. If word spreads, they will definitely be ostracized."

"And what about that scoundrel, Mr. Carter? He should at least be forced to return the racehorse. Or, better still, give it to Tom. He should not have allowed the opportunity to slip through his fingers."

"Isn't anyone concerned about that poor house-maid?" Toodles asked.

"She should definitely be compensated." Henrietta gave a firm nod.

"She will be." Evie shifted to the edge of her chair. "There is something else I've been meaning to tell everyone. It's about Caro…"

Henrietta glanced at Sara. Smiling, she turned to Evie. "Evangeline, you should really practice calling her Lady Evans."

"You know?" Evie looked at the detective who shrugged. If he hadn't told them, then how had they found out?

"Henrietta, I think Evie has had enough mysteries for a while." Sara nudged her. "Tell her."

"Oh, very well. If you must know, the moment the detective expressed an interest in Caro, I made it my business to learn everything I could about him. After all, Caro is one of us." Henrietta gave a firm nod. "We take care of our own."

Sara rolled her eyes. "Henrietta looked him up in Debrett's."

"It's always my first port of call," Henrietta admitted. "Also, the detective bears a striking resemblance to someone I knew in my youth. That triggered my curiosity." She clapped her hands. "A wedding, at long last."

~

Caro is summoned to the drawing room

"I will still be Caro, milady."

"Oh, no, my dear. You have served an apprenticeship as Lady Carolina Thwaites. Now, you will be Lady Evans." Henrietta smiled and gave a nod of approval.

"Get used to it," Toodles said. "Or else, Henrietta will prod you with a stick."

"Practice will make perfect. And now we have a wedding to help plan. Oh, this will be fun. Just think of all the stories you can regale us with."

"Stories?"

"Yes. You know everything that goes on downstairs. Tell us a story now."

"I wouldn't be comfortable telling stories about people I've worked with." Seeing Henrietta's disappointment, Caro exclaimed, "Oh, I know. I can tell you about my experience trying to find another position before I came to work for her ladyship. It was during the season and we were all up in town. I walked past the Mayfair Agency and one of the cards displayed in the window aroused my curiosity. A Mrs. Estelle Harrison required a lady's maid with a special fondness for animals. Well, I grew up in the country and encountered farm animals every day. Also, the Duke's siblings had kept many pets, including a rabbit and a parrot. Anyhow, I felt quite confident I could provide proof of my experience with pets. At the time, I'd pictured a cat or a dog and as I made my way to the appointment, I decided there had to be more than one cat or dog, otherwise why would she have made it a requirement? On the day of my appointment, I set my worries aside and approached the house thinking I could always ask the person who answered the door for more information. To my dismay, the butler merely lifted his nose and told me I would soon find out. I almost had a change of heart but he urged me to come in so I decided it couldn't be at all bad. The butler showed me through to a pretty drawing room decorated in delicate pastel colors." Caro barely drew breath as she continued, "Mrs. Harrison sat in the middle of a chaise lounge. While the weather had turned, the drawing room felt warm so I decided the interview would be quite brief because Mrs. Harrison wore a fur around her neck. That made it look as though she was about to step out for the day."

Caro glanced around the room and noticed everyone's attention still fixed on her.

"Well, go on. Don't keep us in suspense," Henrietta urged. "We have had enough of that to last us a lifetime or at least until the next case."

Nodding, Caro continued, "Mrs. Harrison invited me to sit and proceeded to ask about my previous position. Of course, she was mightily impressed by my posting in the duke's household. After establishing my suitability for the job, she asked about my fondness for animals. I managed to impress her. Very well, she said and asked me to say duchess. Not thinking anything of it, I said it. Well, Mrs. Harrison shook her head and told me to say it louder. At this point, I did begin to wonder about her reasons. I raised my voice slightly and said duchess again. Still, this wasn't good enough for her. That's when I wondered if she was the type to approach titled ladies in the street and would expect me to do it for her if they persisted in ignoring her. Anyhow, I drew in a breath and said it again at the top of my voice. The moment I shouted it, what I thought had been a fur unfurled itself from around her neck, jumped across the room and landed on my lap. I shrieked and threw my arms in the air as she exclaimed, you are frightening my precious monkey."

"A monkey?" Sara exclaimed as Henrietta roared with laughter.

"A marmoset, to be precise. The next day, I received an offer to work with Lady Woodridge, so I had to turn Mrs. Harrison down. I will never know if I would have grown fond of the Duchess."

When Henrietta recovered, she looked at Evie, "Caro gave up the opportunity of working with a monkey to come and work for you. And don't ever forget that, my dear."

Millicent walked in carrying a wrap. Handing it to Caro, she said, "Milady, we wouldn't want you to catch a chill."

"I'm not a lady yet, Millicent."

Henrietta smiled. "Millicent. You must be very happy in your new position."

"Oh, yes, indeed I am, milady. I must admit I have always hoped to someday be Lady Woodridge's maid."

Henrietta looked at Evie and winked. Turning back to Millicent, she asked, "And are you fond of animals? Lady Woodridge is thinking of getting a companion for her new puppy."

∽

Printed in Great Britain
by Amazon